"I'D MARRY A STRANGER!"

Nancy tried hard not to hear another word of the vicious quarrel that was raging beside her. Yet she couldn't help staring at the sensitive, suffering face of the handsome man who proclaimed to his mocking girlfriend, "I'd marry any girl—the first girl I met—rather than marry you as you really are."

Now he sat alone on a bench, helpless, his head in his hands. Swept along by some irresistible impulse, Nancy rushed to his side and touched his strong, clenched hand.

"Did you mean it?" she gasped. *"Will you marry me?"*

EMILIE LORING

A KEY
TO MANY
DOORS

BANTAM BOOKS
TORONTO · NEW YORK · LONDON

A KEY TO MANY DOORS

*A Bantam Book / published by arrangement with
Little, Brown and Company*

PRINTING HISTORY

Little, Brown edition published October 1967

*Bantam edition / August 1970
12 printings through September 1980*

ISBN 0-553-14289-5

Published simultaneously in the United States and Canada

*Bantam Books are published by Bantam Books, Inc. Its trade-
mark, consisting of the words "Bantam Books" and the por-
trayal of a bantam, is Registered in U.S. Patent and Trademark
Office and in other countries. Marca Registrada. Bantam
Books, Inc., 666 Fifth Avenue, New York, New York 10103.*

A KEY TO
MANY DOORS

ONE

THE SHOP, discreet and unostentatious as it appeared from the outside, was one of the most famous in the world. Carefully screened by plainclothes detectives, it admitted only a few customers at a time. Here, but never out of range of watchful eyes, they had displayed before them, in a room that resembled a drawing room rather than a jewelry shop, fantastically beautiful and expensive diamonds.

When Peter Gerard appeared, the manager himself came to greet him, hand outstretched.

"Mr. Gerard! This is a pleasure. We haven't seen you since you selected that diamond engagement ring. I hope the young lady was pleased."

Recalling Cynthia's rapturous exclamation when he had slipped the ring on her slender finger, Peter smiled.

"Peter darling! It's the loveliest thing I ever saw. It's magnificent, and it must be fabulously expensive."

Even at the time he had wished, a trifle uncomfortably, and yet ashamed of feeling any criticism toward his beloved Cynthia, that she had not referred to the money value of the ring.

"It seemed to belong to you, my dearest," he had told her.

"I'll never part with it. Never!" She had flung her arms around his neck and given him one of her rare, cool kisses.

1

"And what," the manager inquired, bringing Peter back to the present, "may we show you today? A gift for the bride?"

"A gift for the bride," Peter agreed.

"A pin? A bracelet? A necklace?"

"A necklace," Peter decided, and the manager beamed.

Attendants brought into the room half a dozen necklaces—there were no display counters in this shop—laid them gently, almost reverently, on black velvet. While Peter inspected them the manager inspected him. He was the third generation of the Gerards to patronize the great diamond merchant, although, until his engagement, he had rarely made purchases, except for gifts for his mother or his cousins. His father and grandfather had long been valued customers of the firm.

There was little of Peter senior in the young man's face or bearing, the manager thought, but no one could mistake his remarkable resemblance to his grandfather: the same broad sweep of forehead, the same heavy dark hair, the same deep-set dark blue eyes under arched brows, the same rather high cheekbones and beautifully shaped mouth, whose expression of gentleness was offset by the firm chin. A fine-looking man, the manager thought. He hoped that the girl with whom Gerard appeared to be so deeply in love would prove to be worthy of him. Men of great inherited wealth who prefer a life of service without striving for power to one of self-indulgent amusement are rare.

"This one," Peter said at length and the manager smiled.

"You remind me more and more of your grandfather, old Simon Gerard. He had an infallible eye. That is probably the most beautiful diamond necklace we have ever handled." He pointed out details. "Naturally, in view of the size and color of the stones, the price—"

Peter lifted a hand to check him. "The groom's gift for the bride. I wanted it perfect."

"Shall we send it to your townhouse, Mr. Gerard, or deliver it to the young lady?"

Peter hesitated for a moment, considering. Then he smiled. It was a smile that transformed his face, making it warmer, younger, irresistibly likable. For a moment something of his father's lighthearted spirit broke through his usual gravity.

"I'm being married tomorrow," he said. "I'll take the necklace with me and give it to her myself."

"It's an extremely valuable thing to carry," the manager said uneasily. "Unless you'd like a guard. We can provide someone."

Peter laughed outright, a joyous ringing laugh. "Good Lord, man, I can take care of myself. Anyhow, I have a feeling that this is my lucky day."

"We'll hope that it is," the manager said, with no answering mirth on his troubled face.

When Peter, the jewel case tucked carefully into an inside pocket of his overcoat, had started briskly down the windswept street, which was beginning to whiten from a light snow, the manager watched his easy stride, his fine carriage, the proud way he carried his head.

"He isn't even driving," he muttered to himself, after looking along the curb for the long sleek black lines of the Gerard town car, for the uniformed driver. "Young men are so reckless. I do hope he'll be careful. Not that anyone would be likely to suspect him of carrying thirty-five thousand dollars worth of diamonds in his pocket. If he has any sense he'll deposit the necklace in a safe as fast as he can."

I

The manager would have been even more perturbed if he could have followed Peter Gerard. Instead of hailing his own car or even a taxi, Peter dived down the stairs of a noisy subway station, wedged his way onto the platform, stood packed against a throng of swaying, pushing men and women, their clothes steaming with wet snow; watched with unseeing eyes the white-tiled stations pass in a blur, unaware of the noise of the train.

Why Brooks had summoned him at all, and summoned him to this preposterous address, baffled him. Why the whole thing had been veiled in secrecy annoyed him. It wasn't like his boss to act like James Bond. For a rising young diplomat the whole thing was ridiculous.

A rising young diplomat. He had, Peter acknowledged to himself, done well. Resisting all his father's persuasions to go into the family business; resisting the more insistent pressures of his playboy acquaintances to devote himself to yachting, skiing, sun-bathing, following the perpetual restless holiday seekers; resisting the deepest pressure of all, his longing to become a painter, he had followed the lines he had marked out for himself.

There were, as he had told his father, any number of men in the organization who could handle the business as well as he could. Probably better, because their hearts were in it. He already had more money than he would ever need. Beyond that, the mere accumulation of money could be only a power drive, and Peter profoundly distrusted men who sought power. What he wanted was to be of service to his world. He had too large a share of its benefits.

Because he had put all his heart and mind and energy into the job, because he had an instinctive sympathy for other peoples, because he was willing to try to understand points of view and ways of life unlike his own, he had risen fast in the diplomatic service.

Now the future stretched clear ahead. In one month he was to embark on the most important assignment he had ever held. True, he had worked for it. Until he had met Cynthia he had not permitted any outside interest to deflect him from his course.

Cynthia! He conjured her up in his mind, small, blond, with soft blue eyes, a small red mouth, a helpless, gentle, dainty creature whom he longed to protect. Cynthia! A smile of delight crept over his face.

Then, as his station flashed into view and the train began to slow, the smile faded. Something about the unaccustomed gravity in Brooks's voice had disturbed him but he had resolutely pushed the feeling aside. Nothing was going to spoil the perfection of this day. In less than two hours, he was going to meet Cynthia and give her the necklace. Tomorrow they would be married. In a month, he would take up his post in one of the great European capitals.

I'll never be this happy again, he thought unexpectedly. I'm on the crest of the wave. This is the peak moment of my life. He pushed his way through the crowd that jostled and shoved its way out of the subway train at Fourteenth Street.

Union Square is a down-at-heels section of New York City. Here, on summer nights, the disgruntled make passionate speeches, attacking the government and making shrill appeals to the passing crowds who rarely pause to listen. The light covering of snow had added no beauty to the dingy spot; it had simply intensified the discomfort.

The address, which Peter had been asked to memorize— "Don't write anything down," he had been warned—was an obscure building, an ancient loft structure, that appeared to be almost uninhabited. An oddly furtive sort of place in which to meet a man like Kendel Brooks. As Peter pushed open the door and closed it behind him, he was aware of a queer kind of premonition that he had taken some momentous step, that nothing would ever be quite the same again.

A shabby, weary-looking old man sat in a worn chair holding a newspaper behind whose shelter he was dozing. After a look at the open-caged, ramshackle elevator, Peter decided not to awaken him and walked up the dirty staircase. There was no name on the door of the room where Brooks waited, but Peter remembered his instructions. It would be the last door on the left on the side of the building facing Fourteenth Street.

Absurd to have this sense of reluctance, but when he knocked on the door and heard Brooks's familiar deep voice call, "Come in," he was relieved. What had he expected, he jeered at himself. A gang of thieves? An opium den? A trap of some sort? He had better curb that imagination.

There were three men sitting at a table in the bleak little room. One of them was Brooks, tall, distinguished, suave. The second was a quiet man so ordinary in appearance that one might pass him a dozen times a day without recognizing him. Something in the unobtrusive blue suit, the bland face that gave away nothing, the eyes that saw everything, alerted Peter. FBI, he thought. What was going on, anyhow? The third man, in late middle age, with thinning hair, a disciplined face, and an air of authority, was known to everyone who read the newspapers or looked at television. If a man of this caliber attended the meeting, something big was in the offing.

For a moment Peter stood quietly, relaxed and at ease, while three pairs of eyes studied him. Then the Personage nodded, and Brooks said, "Glad to see you, Gerard. I am privileged to present you to—" He broke off as the Personage lifted a hand in protest.

"I know the name, sir," Peter said with a smile.

"And Mr. Foster. Mr. Gerard."

"FBI?" Peter asked.

"FBI," the other agreed.

The men shook hands and Peter pulled up the fourth chair. The man from Washington took charge of the meeting. Not one to waste words he talked swiftly, hammering home his points. For the first time Peter understood why he had always been so brilliantly successful in dealing with interviewers, in public debates. He was prepared with the facts and he knew how to marshal and present them clearly.

"This, of course," he concluded, "is not to go beyond this room. Brooks says you are a man whose discretion can be relied upon. We are gambling on the fact that he is showing his usual sound judgment of men."

Peter drew a long breath. "A conspiracy on such a big scale! It's hard to take it in."

There was no reply. The three men were watching him, summing up his reaction to the story, weighing him in the balance.

"Any questions?" the man asked.

"Yes, of course. Why tell me all this, even if you rely on my good faith? What have I to do with it?"

"You have everything to do with it," the other said. "It is true that the material is being mailed in New York, each time from a different borough, but the core of the organization is in a little New England village. Simonton,

Connecticut. Named for your great-grandfather, I believe."

Peter stared at him in disbelief. "That is impossible," he said flatly. "There must be some mistake. There simply couldn't be subversive activities of these gigantic dimensions carried on in Simonton. I know that village the way I know my own hand. I know the people. I—" He broke off as he saw the broad grin on the austere face of the Personage, saw the answering smiles on the faces of Brooks and the self-effacing FBI man.

"That," the Personage said, "is why we need you there, Gerard. As a matter of fact, you are the only possible man for the job. We have no choice."

The silence seemed interminable. Then Peter said quietly, "I think what you mean, sir, is that I have no choice."

There was an awkward pause and then Brooks leaned forward. "Look here, my boy, I've known you all your life. I know your family, your background. I think I know your caliber. I know, too, that what we are asking is a tremendous personal sacrifice. It means that you will relinquish a diplomatic post which you richly deserve; that you will be, in a sense, working underground. A job that carries with it no public credit or reward."

As Peter stared at the table Brooks went on, "You have always believed that service for your country is the most important function you can perform. This service will, I assure you, be far more urgent than any diplomacy you could handle. In a sense, you are the only possible man for the job. As you say yourself, you know the village. You know its people. And what's more important, they know you. Your presence would go unquestioned, while that of an outsider would be bound to arouse curiosity. But—you do have a choice, Gerard. We cannot order you to take this assignment. We merely ask it of you."

At last Peter looked up. To the relief of the three men he was smiling.

"If that's what the country wants of me, I'll do my best."

The man from Washington leaned forward, holding out his hand. "We are grateful, Gerard. Truly grateful. And when the time comes, we will try to show our gratitude in an adequate way. A tangible way. There are other, even bigger, diplomatic posts, you know."

Seeing Peter's discomfiture, Brooks, who knew him well, broke in. "Of course," he said practically, "you'll need some sort of cover. You've got to be able to account for going back to the village this winter, when everyone will expect you to take up your post in Europe."

Peter thought, considering and discarding ideas. "Well," he suggested at length, "I've always longed to be a painter. It's more than a hobby. I have a studio up at the Connecticut house. I could also claim to have some physical disability, if that would help; say that I have to rest for a few months so I'll spend the time devoting myself to painting."

The FBI man nodded. "As long as you know your stuff," he said warningly. "But if they begin to wonder about you, they will have an expert ask questions that might prove embarrassing. As a matter of fact, watch out for anyone who appears to be curious about your presence in Simonton."

"I spent a summer studying in the studio of a first-rate man in Paris. I think I can pass their tests." Peter pinched his lower lip between his fingers while he thought. "Of course," he said at length, "if at any time it should prove—desirable to arouse their suspicions, to draw their fire if I haven't been able to smoke them out in any other way, my physical disabilities could prove to be nonexistent."

"Don't stick your neck out too far," Brooks warned him. "If you need outside help we'll get it to you, but for a case like this it's safer to be a lone wolf. We'll give you a number you can call in an emergency if you should need reinforcements."

"I have a friend up there, best friend I have in the world. If I need help I'll call him in. I'd trust him with my life."

"No," the FBI man said. "No!"

"But—"

"It isn't *your* life," the Personage pointed out, "and you aren't to trust anyone. Is that understood?"

Peter's lips tightened but he nodded his head in agreement.

"Now," the Personage said, smiling faintly, "we come to the most difficult problem. Your wife."

"I'm not married—yet." Peter's smile lighted his face. "I will be tomorrow."

"And what will happen when you tell her of this sudden change in plans?"

"She is going to be disappointed," Peter admitted frankly. "Very much disappointed, I am afraid. She has been building a kind of musical comedy glamour picture of acting as hostess for an ambassador in a great European city. But—we love each other very much, sir. Cynthia will fall in with my plans. I can't conceive of her failing to do that. She'd share anything with me."

"The point is," Brooks pointed out, "that this is something you can't share with her. I am sorry, but that is the way it has to be."

The Personage stood up, indicating that the interview was at an end. Chairs scraped back. "Get up to Simonton as fast as you can, Gerard. Find those men for us and find them in a hurry. We've got to stop this thing. It's building up like a snowball." He shook hands, started for the door, turned back.

"I'm pinning a lot of faith in you. We all are."

TWO

CYNTHIA had agreed somewhat reluctantly to meet Peter in front of the Vermeers at the Metropolitan Museum of Art. She would, he knew, have preferred one of the fashionable cocktail bars but on this one point he had been adamant. As he usually agreed to her wishes without discussion, she had accepted his plan.

Though he would not admit to himself that his lovely Cynthia had any failings, Peter had been disturbed by her liking for cocktails. After they were married, he told himself, that would all change. Meanwhile, he explained tactfully that since their marriage was to be a very quiet one, the service to be performed in the small Manhattan church which the Gerards had supported for generations, it would be unwise for them to be seen together publicly and so arouse the speculations of some gossip columnist. The Gerards, however unostentatiously they might choose to live, were always news.

The private wedding had, to his surprise, been Cynthia's idea. She hated all the fuss and the pictures and the notoriety, she told him, her little hand tucked confidingly under his arm. Wouldn't it be nicer to have a private ceremony and then a honeymoon some place where no one knew them, where they would have only each other? After that, of course, they could announce their marriage publicly.

Peter had been taken aback. Cynthia adored lovely

clothes and all the trappings of wealth. Like a child, he told himself. Like a child. But he had wronged her. She wanted a simple ceremony and she wanted no one but Peter. There had been times when he had wondered uneasily whether she really loved him; she had seemed to endure rather than respond to his kisses, she asked no questions about his work or about himself. But this desire to have him all to herself proved that she did love him, didn't it?

Of course, as an only child, and a very lonely one, she had never learned to share things with anyone. But that would come. A good marriage helped to create a third, a richer, warmer personality. It did not diminish two personalities. That was what his marriage was going to be.

Nonetheless, as Peter hailed a cab and asked the driver to take him to the Metropolitan Museum, he was deeply troubled. He was going to inflict a heavy disappointment on Cynthia and he hated to do it. He directed the driver of the cab to the parking lot behind the Museum.

"You want me to wait?" the driver asked in surprise.

"No, I just want to see whether my car is here."

He had offered Cynthia the use of his car because she took a childlike delight in its luxury, in having a uniformed man take her orders. The sleek black Rolls had been parked and the driver was sitting at the wheel, industriously reading a paperback edition of a book on politics. Max was a demon for self-improvement and he had tried to put himself through college the hard way, by going to night school.

The chauffeur closed his book, snapped to attention, and started to open the door when he caught sight of his employer. Peter shook his head and Max let down the window, looking out inquiringly.

"Been here long?" Peter asked, his voice casual, but feeling anxious because he was a quarter of an hour late and he remembered that Cynthia did not like to be kept waiting.

"Just five minutes, sir. Miss Barbee had some shopping to do."

"Good. We won't be long."

As he went up the long flight of steps to the museum

entrance, Peter found his heart racing. Poor Cynthia, she was going to be so disappointed. As though to encourage himself, he touched his pocket, feeling the jewel case inside. At least, she would love the necklace.

For a moment, as he entered the gallery with the Vermeers, he stood transfixed, as always, by the miracle of the artist's workmanship. How the man had understood the use of light, known that light was the greatest painter of them all.

He shifted his position to view the familiar canvas better, and to see around the girl who stood looking at it. There was something curiously familiar about her; then he realized that she resembled a Renaissance madonna that he had once copied: smooth black hair parted in the middle, large dark eyes, an oval face. Even the blue of her dress under the plain black coat seemed to fit the illusion. Or was it the hopeless despair in the droop of her mouth, the tragic eyes? No, he told himself, there had been an acceptance of grief in the Renaissance madonna. This girl had a kind of controlled desperation in her manner.

He turned away, feeling that he had no right to spy on her personal tragedy. Cynthia, seated on a bench, was not looking at pictures. She was examining her face in a compact and the angle of the tiny red hat perched on blond curls. She looked like an illustration on an old-fashioned candy box, except that she was not smiling. One small foot in its absurd wisp of a shoe with a four-inch heel was tapping impatiently.

"Darling," he said, "I'm sorry to keep you waiting. There was an unexpected but very important conference."

"There always seems to be an important conference." The enticing red mouth drooped sullenly.

"Sorry." He smiled at her, took her hand in his. "But this is the last of it. Tomorrow—"

She gave him a dazzling smile. "I know. I keep pinching myself to make myself believe it. Tomorrow I'll be married. Peter, my sweet, I've been thinking."

"Have you indeed, my pet?" How natural it seemed to treat her like the child she was.

"The cold is so ghastly. I hate it! Can't we go to Bermuda, maybe Monte Carlo, or somewhere that's smart and fashionable for our honeymoon? Somewhere gay." As he made no comment she reached out a small hand to stroke his cheek, her usual gesture of affection. "After all, it's not as though you couldn't afford it! And today I saw the most ravishing winter cruise outfits. Oh, Peter, they were heavenly!"

For a moment he stared blankly at the picture on the wall facing them, a Dutch interior, the placid woman, the light pouring through an open window. He did not see it. What he saw was a grimy room on Fourteenth Street and three anxious faces watching him.

"Darling," he said at last, "I'm terribly sorry. Perhaps next winter. But now—"

"There's only one honeymoon, you know, Peter. What do they say in the advertisements? 'Accept no substitutes.' I want my sunny honeymoon now." There was unexpected steel behind the soft voice.

"Darling," he began again, "I wish we could go to Bermuda, Monte Carlo, wherever you like, but something—that is, we can't go now. And with you it will be a sunny honeymoon, anywhere, my dearest."

The impatient foot tapped more quickly. "Where are we going?"

"My home town. Well, it's a village really. Simonton, Connecticut." When she made no reply he looked at her anxiously. "It's an old family house and I think you'll like it."

"Shut up in a bleak New England village in the wintertime! I think you're out of your mind, Peter. A dead-and-alive place. Cold and snow and ice and bad roads and nothing to do. What are you afraid of?" Her voice had grown shrill. "Do you think I'll have a cocktail when you aren't looking? Do you—"

"Steady." His hand closed over hers. "Not so loud," he said in a low voice. "People can hear you."

She looked around. "There's no one here but a girl who looks like a zombie and a guard at the door who doesn't care as long as we don't harm his precious pictures. Pictures!" she exclaimed viciously. "Who wants to look at a lot of dull old things like those?"

"Cynthia!" His eyes were imploring.

Her eyes watched him with unexpected shrewdness, with cold calculation. "What's the real scoop, Peter? Don't you think I'm fit to be a diplomat's wife? Do you plan to spend our honeymoon having me taught how to act properly or something?"

He had unbuttoned his overcoat when he entered the museum. Now he reached for the jewel case. His hand dropped. He did not want her on those terms. He did not want to buy her allegiance.

"Something came up today," he said at last. If only he could bridge this bitter misunderstanding by telling her the truth! But he had been so sure, so blindly sure, that she would share anything with him without question. "My doctor," and he hated the lie, "says I must have a long rest before I do any further work. He suggested that I go home and take up my hobby, painting. In time, of course, I'll be perfectly well. You must understand that. I'm not asking you to marry an invalid."

"How much time?" she asked. She did not, he realized, seem interested in what might be wrong with him physically. She didn't seem interested in him. Period.

"I don't know. It depends on—circumstances."

"A month? More than a month?" There was something inexorable in her voice, something hard in the blue eyes that watched.

"I don't know," he said helplessly.

"And the diplomatic post?"

He forced a smile. "I'm afraid that's out, Cynthia, at least for the time being. But some day there will be another post, another—"

"Some day!" She drew a long breath. "Listen to me, Peter. I set my heart on marrying a diplomat, on being hostess, on being important. I don't intend to bury myself in a hick village in the winter, watching the snowplow go by for my daily excitement. I'm young. I'm pretty. I want life. If you're going to shut yourself up in the old family homestead you'll do it alone. Is that clear?"

For a long moment they looked at each other. Slowly he began to draw on his gloves. "Quite clear."

"I don't know what your doctor said, but you look like a pretty healthy specimen to me. And you're ambitious.

I'm no fool, Peter. I'd never marry a playboy just because he was rich. That kind has so many lawyers around him, sewing things up, that a girl wouldn't get anywhere. But you have full control of the Gerard money, it's free and clear. Between you and me, my sweet, that's all you have. You aren't my type. No life in you. No sense of fun. No kicks. But I'll play along if you will play my way."

"I can't play your way, Cynthia."

Her red mouth curved in its enchanting smile. "I'll give you a month," she said confidently, "to think things over and then, when you crawl back and say you'll take that diplomatic post, we'll talk about it again."

He stood up. He was colorless but his voice was quiet. Too quiet. "I will never crawl back, Cynthia."

"You're too much in love to give me up."

"I was in love with a dream, not with you as I see you now."

"You'll find that there's nothing to do in a New England village in the wintertime except dream," she mocked him with unshaken confidence in her influence over this man who had adored her. "And you're going to dream about me."

"Don't make any mistake about it," Peter said, his eyes cold and bleak. "I'd marry any girl—the first girl I met—rather than marry you as you really are."

She smiled, lifted her hand to stroke his cheek. Unexpectedly her sharp nail dug a deep scratch. "We'll see, my sweet."

With a staccato tapping of high heels she went out of the gallery, leaving behind her a scent of perfume, leaving desolation and disillusionment and emptiness.

Rather than follow her out of the building—crawling back, she would think—Peter sat down on the bench as though his knees had given way. As he shifted position, he was aware of the jewel case in his pocket. The diamond necklace!

He was numb with shock. He had built his future around the girl who had just left the gallery, who had literally walked out of his life. He would never call her back. Never crawl. For what? For a dream that was gone, for a girl who had never existed outside his imagination.

Cynthia had made that clear. He wasn't her type. She had made sure he had full control of the Gerard money. For that she had been prepared to endure him.

As someone sat down on the bench beside him he started to get up. He needed to be alone.

"Oh, please don't go!" The voice was dismayed; it was also as rounded and beautiful as a low-toned bell.

He turned to see the girl who had reminded him of a turbulent Renaissance madonna, a madonna with banked fires; a contradiction in terms which was absurd.

She faced him as though braced for catastrophe. Her eyes were terrified.

"Did you mean it?" she asked.

"Mean what?" He spoke vaguely, wishing that the tiresome girl would go away, take her troubles elsewhere. He had enough troubles of his own.

"That you would marry the first girl you met?"

His voice was suddenly hard. "What's that got to do with you?"

"Well, I wondered—in that case—will you marry me?"

THREE

UNLIKE MOST physicians, Dr. Warburton took his own advice. Having diagnosed his trouble as a result of extreme fatigue, he had spent a lazy month cruising among the Greek Islands. Now he stood, bronzed and fit, staring down at his patient. He was appalled as he observed the changes that those weeks had made in the man. When he had gone away he had been convinced that Neil—Noah, he corrected himself, he must remember that the patient had signed in at the hospital under the name of Noah Jones—was well on the road to recovery. Now he seemed to have lost all desire to live, the will that can accomplish more than any doctor in restoring health.

Dr. Warburton went over in his mind the background of the case. Some months earlier, Jones and his wife had been driving slowly along a country lane, enjoying the scenery. A car traveling at terrific speed had sideswiped theirs. Jones's wife had been killed outright. Jones himself had suffered from a variety of internal injuries and his face had been badly disfigured by broken glass. The internal injuries were healing satisfactorily and a brilliant plastic surgeon had begun work on his face.

Now he sat listlessly in a big armchair near the window, a blanket drawn up over his knees, a skeleton-thin hand lying on an unopened book. His eyes were lackluster. His voice was dull. He had lost a great deal of weight.

He answered the doctor's questions without interest.

17

What, in heaven's name, had happened to him, the doctor wondered in dismay.

Warburton assumed a hearty tone. "You know, Neil— uh, Noah—you have a smart doctor. I took my own advice. After a month looking at new sights and doing nothing I feel like a new man."

"Oh, you've been away?" Noah said indifferently.

The doctor looked at him sharply. Had there been some head injury that had gone undetected? "The Greek Islands. One of the world's more rewarding experiences. That's my prescription for you. Get out of this hospital room. Take one of these cruises and I'll guarantee—"

"No!" It was the first time there had been any feeling in the man's voice. Now he sounded frenzied. "Go on a cruise where people can see me like this? Never! I—"

"All right." Dr. Warburton's voice was quiet. "There's no need to get yourself all worked up. If you don't want to go you don't have to go. It was just an idea of mine. It worked for me and I thought it might work for you."

He stood looking down at his patient, the milky daylight on Noah's face revealing the extent of the scars. It was a mess, of course. But after another operation and when the scars had faded, the face would be almost entirely normal. Neil—Noah, Warburton reminded himself—had been one of the handsomest men he had ever met. It would be a great pity if he were disfigured for life. Not that there was much chance of it.

After his outburst Noah had relapsed into his former apathy.

"Just the same," the doctor said, "you won't get well this way, sitting in a chair, brooding. You've simply got to get out of this hsopital, get yourself in shape to go back to your old job."

Noah looked at him, looked down again, his thin fingers plucking at the blanket over his knees. "I'll never be able to go back," he said. "I can't remember. I try— but a few minutes later it's just a blank."

Warburton, from long practice, held the confident smile on his lips. "That's perfectly natural. Nothing at all to worry about. In fact, you must not worry about it; do not try to remember." He ignored the other man's impatient gesture. "I mean that. Let nature heal you. One of these days it will be like a curtain rolling back."

Noah shrugged, dismissing this cheerful comment as an empty promise.

"What are you reading?" the doctor asked, changing the subject, trying to gauge the state of the man's mind.

Noah turned the book on his lap, looking for the title. "Oh, yes. *Henry the Fourth*. Nancy's been reading to me."

"Somehow I've seen very little of your charming sister. She must be quite a girl."

"She is. She flew back from Switzerland as soon as she heard of the accident. I don't think there's a day she hasn't been with me and just as long as the hospital staff allowed, except when I was undergoing surgery or having tests and treatments. She has been wonderful. I told her that it wasn't necessary but she insists. As she says, she has never really had a family before, and she is making up for lost time."

"That's right." The doctor caught eagerly at a subject which seemed to hold his apathetic patient's interest. "You're the only members of the family, aren't you?"

"Yes, our parents died when Nancy was only ten. I was nearly twelve years older and I'd got rather an early start."

"I remember." The doctor grinned.

"Well, of course, I couldn't keep Nancy with me. That's no life for a little girl, not a normal environment, so I picked out the best schools I could find in England and France and Switzerland. As a result, I was able to see her only at long intervals. Sometimes I wouldn't be able to get away for nearly a year. So now, as she says, we are making up for lost time, getting acquainted with each other at last."

"But what are Nancy's own interests? Apart from you, I mean?"

"Why—" Noah stared blankly at the doctor. "I don't know. Probably I have been too self-centered. She has no friends in this country." After a long interval he said slowly, "I have been inexcusably selfish. Somehow, I just took Nancy for granted."

Again Warburton's keen eyes surveyed the sick man. There was a new light in them. What you need, young man, he thought to himself, is to forget your troubles and consider someone else. That will be your salvation.

I

In a little alcove not far from her brother's room, Anne Jones, Nancy to her friends, was waiting for the doctor's verdict. After many months she had become accustomed to hospital smells, to the swift silent movements of doctors and nurses, to the silent rolling of rubber-tired stretchers carrying patients back and forth, to the anxiety-ridden relations and friends who waited, as she was waiting now, for a doctor's verdict. Except that in this case there were no friends. The man who was registered as Noah Jones never had any visitors except for his sister.

It seemed to Nancy that there was no bridge between her past and her present. For ten years she had moved from one school to another, from one country to another, learning new languages, making new friends, moving on before the friendships could grow deep and meaningful. With the exception of a few girls from broken homes, they all had a family to go to during their vacations.

For Nancy, vacation time always meant a trip arranged by her brother to a new country, carefully chaperoned by an older woman who made sure that every moment was devoted to learning about the country, its language, its history and culture, its churches and monuments, especially its art. The one place her brother had never thought of her visiting was her own country.

Now and then, but so rarely, he made one of his fleeting appearances, filling the girls with wild excitement because of his good looks and his great charm. For Nancy he had revealed only a careless brotherly affection; she had been aware that she was not important in his life; she was simply a duty to be performed as well and as generously as possible.

Because she had no devoted family, no close girl friends, and she had been permitted to meet very few men, she had never thought of herself as belonging to anyone. She was just Nancy.

In the beginning, in spite of her shock over the accident and the tragic death of the sister-in-law whom she had never met, Nancy had rejoiced that at last there was something for her to do, some need for her to fill. For a while her gay courage, her resolute optimism had fanned the small spark of hope in her brother, helped him surmount his grief over his wife's loss, helped him believe that eventually he could go back to his old life.

Then several weeks later, she had come in to find him staring at her blankly.

"I can't remember," he told her.

"Remember what?"

"Anything. I tried to repeat some lines, some verses, and they just—they're gone. My memory's gone."

Nancy had met his despairing eyes confidently. "Then," she told him, "we'll get it back."

If only she could feel as confident as she sounded! Just the same, she told herself, we'll fight this out if it takes all summer. Or, in this case, all winter. She looked at the windowpane, which was being starred by snow, and shivered, not with cold but with fear. Suppose I fail, she thought.

She started as a hand touched her shoulder lightly.

"Miss Jones! You're jittery as a nervous horse." Dr. Warburton looked down at her, smiling. "Here, let me look at you, girl. What have you been doing to yourself?"

She gave a warning glance toward her brother's door which the doctor had carelessly left open.

He did not seem to notice. "Lost weight, haven't you?"

"A little."

"How much? Five pounds? Ten?"

"Twelve, but I feel all right."

"You don't look it, so don't argue with me. You are worn out, on edge, too thin. You are trying to carry your brother through the doldrums by sheer will power."

"I'm helping him. Really I am."

The doctor studied her. A curious face, a memorable face, he thought, with its oval perfection of shape, its great dark eyes, its warm mouth revealing humor and generosity

and a passionate nature that slept, unaware of its poten-
tialities. It wasn't usual for so lovely a girl to fail to
exploit her own attractions. It was high time that someone
discovered her, that she left her brother to find his own
salvation and developed the qualities that would make her
a rare person. He found himself envying the fortunate
man who would win this woman's love.

"Of course you're helping him. But don't overdo it."

"What do you mean by that?"

"In the first place, some of this burden has to be carried
by—uh, Noah himself. You can't do it all for him. In the
second place, you have a life of your own to live. You are
twenty and so far you haven't even started. It's high time
you did."

"I don't matter."

The doctor grinned at her. "You matter a lot more than
you realize, a lot more than your brother realizes. You're
a very pretty girl and you have an exceptional capacity for
loving and giving. Don't waste it, my dear."

"And what about Noah's memory? Did he tell you?"

"It will come back when he wants it to come back. No,
don't get angry. He is running away from something in his
mind. When he can accept it, his memory will return."

"He has lost a lot of ground lately," she said anxiously.
"You must see that, Doctor."

"Get him out of that hospital room and find him a new
interest."

"But he won't see people!"

"Somehow, you will find a way. But just remember that
Nancy counts, too."

II

When Nancy returned to her brother's room she gave a
startled exclamation. Noah had flung off the blanket, he
was standing beside the bed, holding on to it for support,
shaking.

"Noah! What's the matter?"

While the frantic words poured out she stood appalled.
He had overheard what Dr. Warburton had told her.

Remembering that open door Nancy realized in a flash of insight and indignation that, for some reason of his own, the doctor had intended her brother to overhear.

The wild, tortured words went on and on. Noah was destroying her life. She had always been an exile from her own people, her own country, on his account. She was a living sacrifice to him. If that was the case, he'd be better off dead. Because of him she had no home, she had no friends.

A vague idea occurred to Nancy but she brushed it aside. He would never believe her. And sooner or later, he would learn the truth.

In vain she tried to stop Noah's torrent of words, to calm him. Finally, when he was exhausted, she eased him into his chair, pulled the blanket up over his knees. He lay back, eyes closed, spent by the emotional storm, the scars clearly visible on his face.

What shall I do? What shall I do? The words beat ceaselessly on her mind. If she left Noah now, he would give up the struggle to get well. More clearly than the doctor, she recognized the strain of weakness in her brother's character that required a stronger will to lean on. Not that she condemned him. Not that it altered her devotion to him. He was as he was.

But how could she stay? The doctor had convinced Noah that she was sacrificing her life and he rejected the sacrifice.

She knelt beside him, holding his thin, cold fingers in her warm hands. For once in her life she had to act and it had to be good. My first appearance on any stage, she thought, and the idea brought a smile to her lips, a sparkle to her eyes.

"Now," she said, smiling at him, "if you'll just stop behaving like an idiot, I'll tell you a secret. I've been waiting to tell you for a long time but when you were seriously ill and, later, when you had that temporary memory loss—"

"Temporary?" he said bitterly.

"That's the wrong question," she said gaily. "You are supposed to ask—what secret?"

For the first time he smiled at her in his old way. "What secret, mysterious lady?"

"I'm engaged to be married."

"You're what!"

She laughed spontaneously. "Your surprise is hardly flattering. Did you suppose that no man would want to marry me?"

"Of course not." He sounded bewildered. "But I didn't know you even had any friends in America. I must say you've been neglecting this man for me. He must be the soul of patience or," he grinned mischievously, "he can't be much in love with you."

She tilted back her head challengingly. "He adores me."

"Tell me about this lucky fellow."

She shook her head. "After that big scene of yours you have about had it for today. I'll ring for the nurse to put you back to bed where you belong. Tomorrow, I'll tell you all about him." She rang the bell for the nurse, blew a kiss to her brother, and went out, closing the door behind her.

What shall I do? The question accompanied her down in the elevator, out into the street, where she stood for a moment looking out at the East River and north toward Gracie Mansion, the charming old landmark which was the official residence of the Mayor of New York City. A sharp wind flung snow in her face but she drew the air gratefully into her lungs. After the overheated hospital, with its inevitable smells of ether and medications, the air felt fresh and clean. As clean, that is, as New York air can ever be.

She turned up her collar, thrust her hands into the deep pockets of her coat, and began aimlessly to walk west.

Through the cacophony of New York she walked, deaf to the drills, the throbbing of motors, the impatient blare of horns. Through crowded streets she walked, blind to the bumper-to-bumper traffic, to thronged sidewalks, to exotic window displays in smart shops. She turned unseeingly onto Fifth Avenue, walked under the canopies of famous hotels and lavish apartment buildings, where uniformed doormen whistled for taxis and opened car doors for tenants.

What shall I do?

She blinked the blinding snow off her eyelashes and forced herself to think. A wise teacher had once told her, "If you can state your problem clearly you are on the road to solving it."

Well, what was the problem? First, she had to get Noah out of the hospital, in spite of his morbid shrinking from people. Second, she had to find him a new interest, a challenge that would make him forget his own problems. Third, she had to provide a plausible explanation for the invisible fiancé. Because, if she could not, she faced an insurmountable obstacle. Noah would refuse to let her help him any longer. He was determined that she must have a life of her own. So—she seemed to have come full circle.

One thing she must do at once. She must create a convincing story about her engagement to account for the fact that her fiancé had never put in an appearance, that he did not seem to object to her spending all her time with her brother.

I'll explain that we met and became engaged in Switzerland, she decided. I'll say that he plans to join me here in two or three months' time, when we'll be married. Meanwhile, there would be no reason why I can't go on looking after Noah. And by then, he'll be well enough to go on by himself. He won't need me any longer. Then I can pretend to break off the engagement.

She tested the story. So far as she could tell, it sounded convincing.

The snow was deeper now and the thin soles of her shoes had soaked through. She was aware that she was thoroughly chilled and that she was tired. Terribly tired. Without realizing it, she had walked for miles.

Across Fifth Avenue was the Metropolitan Museum of Art and, when the light changed, Nancy crossed the street and climbed the steps wearily. Inside, she dropped down on a bench, vaguely aware of the people who moved from the checking booth to the counter where catalogs and

reproductions were sold, and on to the great flight of stairs
that led to the galleries of paintings.

After a moment of indecision, she went in search of the
seventeenth-century Dutch paintings. Today, she felt a
need of their sunlit sanity. At least, she could sit down
until she was really rested and at the same time look at
beauty.

She smiled as she passed the guard at the door, saw a
girl sitting before a Vermeer, fumbling for her compact.
How pretty she is, Nancy thought, with her blond hair
and her delicate features. The girl looked up as though she
were waiting for someone, and Nancy was taken aback by
the unexpected shrewdness in the cold blue eyes that
summed her up from head to foot and dismissed her as of
no importance.

Nancy stood looking at the painting. Then she heard
rapid footsteps and a man came into the gallery, glanced
at the painting, at Nancy, and then turned toward the
small blond girl, his face alight.

"Darling," he said, "I'm sorry to keep you waiting."

At something in his warm face, the expression of his
eyes, the sound of deep devotion in his voice, Nancy felt
as though a giant hand had squeezed her heart. How the
man loved the little blond girl! How sweet, how wonderful, it must be to be loved like that!

It did not occur to her that she was eavesdropping.
Even when she heard the little blonde describe her as a
girl who looked like a zombie, it made no impression. At
least, not at the time. Something held her rooted as the
girl in the red hat, the girl with the cold eyes, lashed out
with swift cruel words like slashing knives, making clear
that she planned to marry the man only for his money.
She didn't even pretend concern that he had some physical disability. She did not bother to ask what it was.

You aren't my type. Even then, even when she had
hurt him in every possible way, she was sure of him.
*When you crawl back. You're too much in love to give me
up.*

Perhaps she was right, though the man, brightness gone
from his face, white to the lips, said, "I'd marry any

girl—the first girl I met—rather than marry you as you really are."

The girl's nail had dug a deep gash down his cheek. "We'll see, my sweet."

It seemed to Nancy that something had taken possession of her, that she acted without plan. She went to take the place on the bench which the blond girl had vacated. As the man started to get up, she exclaimed, "Oh, please don't go!"

He looked at her as though he barely saw her, an annoyance to get rid of. The zombie.

"Did you mean it?" she asked.

"Mean what?"

"That you would marry the first girl you met?"

He was angry now. He dabbed with a handkerchief at the blood oozing from the scratch on his cheek. "What's that got to do with you?"

"Well, I wondered—in that case—will you marry me?"

FOUR

AN HOUR later, over tea and little sandwiches in a quiet corner of a famous hotel, Peter sat back and, with her permission, lighted his pipe. The scratch on his face still showed as a red, angry mark, but it had stopped bleeding. In the past hour Nancy had seen a number of expressions on his face: happiness and hope, shock and disbelief, disillusionment and the humiliation and pain that had come with the revelation of the woman he loved.

Since then his mood had fluctuated from anger at her knowledge of his humiliation, to surprise, and now, unexpectedly, to amusement.

"All right, young lady, let's have it. So far you have told me a pack of lies. All very interesting," he grinned, "but highly improbable."

"I know," she admitted candidly. "I'm not a good liar."

He laughed outright. Seeing his face alight she wondered what kind of man the blond girl could possibly prefer.

"How old are you?" he asked.

"Twenty."

"What's your name?" As she hesitated he laughed again. "It's customary, you know, to be acquainted with the person you ask to marry you."

The girl flushed scarlet but she met his eyes steadfastly. "My name is Anne Jones."

"Jones. Well, it has the advantage of being well known."

Sparks of anger appeared in her dark eyes like twin candles. "It really is Jones. After all, people are named Jones."

"Indeed they are. And what do your friends usually call you?"

"Nancy."

"And why do you want to marry me, Nancy?" he asked gravely, but with amusement in his eyes.

"Oh, I don't!" she exclaimed.

Then he sobered. "I never expected to be laughing like this. I'll say one thing for you, Nancy, you have a way of distracting a man from his problems. Now be a good girl, tell me what sort of game you've been playing, and I'll send you home before it gets any later. Your family will be worried."

"I haven't any family. At least I have—and that's the trouble."

He shook his head. "I suppose you know what you are talking about."

"The only family I have is an older brother. Nearly a year ago, he was in an automobile accident. His wife was killed. He was badly injured and his face was," she steadied her voice, "terribly scarred. I came as soon as I could, and, for a while, he got better. Then," she made a helpless gesture, "just all of a sudden he lost incentive or something. Today, I talked with his doctor. He says my brother should be taken out of the hospital, somewhere quiet, where he won't need to see people, and where he can get back his will to live."

She looked across the table to see whether her companion was interested. He was watching her, a curious expression on his face.

"Go on," he said.

"What caused all the trouble was that my brother overheard the doctor tell me that I was being sacrificed. He—just fell apart. He won't let me help any more—and he needs me. So I told him I really did have a life of my own, and that I was going to be married."

She sketched out the story she had prepared. "It's a very convincing story, don't you think?"

"Very. What I can't understand is why you aren't able to produce a real fiancé."

"I've hardly met any men," she admitted. "I've been away at boarding schools. So—" This time she was silent for minutes. He made no effort to help her. The amused interest had faded from his face. He had withdrawn so far that she did not know how to reach him.

She expelled a long breath and squared her shoulders, but she did not attempt to look at him. She knew that she would be touching a raw wound.

"So—I was in the Museum—" She came to a full stop.

"As I understand it," he said harshly, "after hearing Cynthia jilt me, you thought it would be a nice idea for you to take her place."

"Oh, no!" she cried, shocked. "That never occurred to me. All I thought—and I see now what a stupid thing it was—I thought I could pretend to my brother, just for a little while, until he's on the way to recovery and won't worry about me, that we are engaged, as long as you—as long—" Her voice faded, was clear again. "You see, I just don't know anyone else. I'm not a good liar, so I thought if I could produce a real fiancé it would be more convincing. That's all."

He sat holding his pipe, looking at nothing.

"Well," she said shakily, "thank you for the tea. I'm quite warm now and my shoes are dry. Good-by and—good luck, Mr.—"

"Peter Gerard," he said absently. "Wait. Don't go yet."

"The waiter has been hovering for the last fifteen minutes," she told him.

Peter seemed to snap out of a dream, he looked for the waiter who approached with alacrity and relief to present the bill. They walked in silence toward the big doors which a uniformed doorman leaped to open for them, saluting Peter in pleased recognition. The Rolls was at the curb.

"I'll take you home," Peter offered. "You'll never get a

cab during the rush hour on a stormy night like this. What's the address?"

"I have a furnished room near the hospital. I don't have a home here. I haven't lived in America since I was ten."

"Doesn't your brother have a place of some kind?"

"His home is—was—in California for a couple of years before his accident. He was on vacation when his car was smashed, and his wife was killed."

Abruptly Peter asked, "What's the name of your brother's physician?"

"Dr. Warburton."

"Not Ross Warburton?"

"Yes, do you know him?"

"I know of him. He has a sound reputation."

"Oh, he's doing his best." Nancy leaned back in the luxurious car, conscious only of her fatigue. Never before had she felt so completely exhausted, so spent. Oddly enough, she was not embarrassed. What this man, this Peter Gerard, might think of her did not matter. She had grasped at a straw, obeyed an impulse, and she had been wrong. Nothing seemed to matter now.

"Look here," Peter said, "you are worn out. If you are living in a furnished room I'll bet you don't even intend to bother with dinner tonight. You probably think those dinky little sandwiches will carry you through until breakfast tomorrow."

"I'm not hungry."

"Well, you've got to eat." As she started to protest, he said, "For your brother's sake. It won't help him if you collapse."

"I won't collapse," she said indignantly.

He gave an order to the chauffeur. "I'm taking you home with me for dinner. After all, if you are going to be engaged, you might as well see the place."

It was a moment before the meaning of the words penetrated her tired mind. She straightened up. "You mean you would—you will play along? Pretend for a month or two?"

"We'll talk it over," Peter said.

I

The house was on Sixty-eighth Street between Fifth and Madison Avenues, a four-story building, its heavy plate-glass door protected by an outer door of lacy but sturdy iron grill-work.

The butler who admitted them was less formidable than Nancy had anticipated, a middle-aged man with a round merry face on which his imposed dignity sat rather comically.

At Peter's suggestion, he took the girl upstairs where a friendly maid showed her the powder room. As Nancy ran her fingers wearily through her hair, the maid said, "Would you like me to brush your hair and massage your scalp? I used to do it for Mr. Peter's mother when she had a headache. She said it helped more than all the headache powders."

"I'd love it," Nancy exclaimed.

While she lay on a chaise longue, the maid deftly took down her hair, giving a little exclamation of admiration as it fell to her waist like a soft black cloud.

"What beautiful hair," the maid said, and her fingers began moving over Nancy's scalp, down the back of her neck, where the muscles were sore and stiff from tension. After a few minutes Nancy closed her eyes, surrendering herself to the healing hands that brought comfort to her throbbing head.

"Dinner will be served in fifteen minutes," the maid said, smiling, and Nancy sat up with a start.

"What—what time is it?"

"Quarter past seven. You've slept nearly an hour and a half." The maid beamed at her.

"Good heavens. I didn't mean to do that."

"I told Mr. Peter you had fallen asleep. He said to let you rest until the last minute."

She watched while Nancy arranged her hair with its smooth center part, combed sleekly and severely. Only a beauty would dare wear her hair like that, the maid thought, but somehow it was right for the pure oval of the girl's face.

When Nancy was shown into the drawing room, Peter got up from an easy chair before the fire.

"Feel better?" he asked.

"Much better. I didn't expect to fall asleep."

"Best thing for you."

Over dinner, with the butler and a waitress in the room, he kept the conversation casual, impersonal. They might, she thought, have been old friends. Then she realized that was the impression he was deliberately conveying to his staff. Perhaps, after all—

She looked across the table to meet his eyes. They were bleak and tired, however light his voice might be. She wondered what thoughts had been going through his mind while she slept. One thing she was sure of, they had not been pleasant.

"We'll have coffee in my mother's morning room," he said, when he had come to pull back her chair.

The room was small and gay, with fresh flowers, cheerful chintz and a fire crackling on the hearth. Over the mantel was the portrait of a woman of fifty. She wasn't beautiful but she had great dignity softened by compassion and humor. Her eyes smiled.

For a moment Nancy stood looking at it. "What a lovely person!"

"My mother? Yes, she was. I've tried to keep this room just as she left it. Except for the portraits, of course. While she was alive, she had a painting of father there. It's in the library now."

The girl still stood before the portrait. "It's beautiful work, isn't it? Masterly. And yet I don't seem to recognize the style. Who is the painter?" She leaned closer, searching for the name of the artist.

"I did it about five years ago," Peter said.

She turned toward him, eyes shining with excitement. "You! I didn't know. I didn't even recognize your name." She repeated, "Peter Gerard," as though questioning her memory, and shook her head.

He gave her a searching look. She might be a bad liar, as she claimed. Certainly she sounded honest enough about his name. She did not appear to associate him with the Gerard fortune, but if she had overheard Cynthia's comments—he winced as he thought of them—if she had noticed the Rolls, if she had paid any attention to the townhouse and its furnishings, she must know he was a man of considerable means.

"Where do you exhibit?" she asked.

"I don't." Remembering his new role he added quickly, "I'm going to work hard this winter and prepare for a one-man show in the spring."

"You're good," she said slowly. "Better than good."

"Do paintings interest you?"

"I think I've seen every famous painting in free Europe," she told him. "At least, everything but the ones in private collections. Not that it makes me a connoisseur, of course; just an enthusiast."

He took out his pipe, looking questioningly at her, lighted it. "Cigarette?"

"Thanks, I don't smoke."

"Brandy with your coffee?"

She shook her head. "I'm afraid I'm not the sophisticated type. This is the first time in my life I've been out on my own, unchaperoned, incredible as it must seem."

"Why?"

She found herself telling him about her years in private European schools, her vacations, spent for the most part in museums.

"It sounds rather lonely," he commented.

"I don't think my brother realized that. Anyhow, he was strongly convinced that I should be kept, as far as possible, away from his kind of world."

Peter waited, but she had no more information to offer. After a long silence he tapped out his pipe.

"While you were asleep," he said abruptly, "I made a couple of telephone calls. One of them was to Dr. Ross Warburton. He confirms your story."

"Confirms!" Spots of color burned in her cheeks. "Did you think I was lying to you?"

He laughed. "After all," he said reasonably, "you've done a good bit of lying to me, haven't you?" Without waiting for an answer he went on. "Warburton agrees that your brother should get out of the hospital, learn to meet people in spite of his temporary disfigurement, which, he says, will probably be overcome by a final bit of plastic surgery and time for the scars to disappear. He also said your brother ought to begin to take an interest in something more than his own woes."

The dry, almost contemptuous, tone in which he spoke infuriated Nancy. What right had he to judge, to be so scornful? But innate honesty made her acknowledge painfully to herself that Peter Gerard was probably making a faithful report of Dr. Warburton's frank opinion.

"All in all," Peter went on, "I am prepared to take you up on your rather peculiar proposition." As she started to speak, he gestured sharply with his hand and she was silent, resentful, fuming. Who did he think he was, anyhow? Of all the dominating, rude, heartless men she had ever encountered, he was the worst.

"What I am suggesting," Peter went on, perfectly aware of her smoldering indignation, completely unmoved by it, "is a bargain. A fair bargain, I hope. You'll present me to your brother tomorrow as your fiancé who has just arrived from Europe. You can say," his voice was dry, "I was too impatient to wait any longer for you. We'll take him up to Simonton as soon as we are married. There's a guesthouse on the grounds which he can have so that he will be alone if he chooses to be. I'll provide a male nurse for him. We'll find something to interest him, if he can't do it for himself."

Only one part of his speech registered with Nancy. "Married?" she said blankly.

"This is where the bargain comes in, Nancy. I'm going to look after your brother; I'll trust you, in return, to honor my name. I'll see that you have an adequate income after we have the marriage annulled. But in the meantime —"

She shrank back in her chair, her heart thudding. She had no idea of how she looked, her great dark eyes tormented, her soft mouth trembling. Peter ignored her panic.

"You are going to have to earn this, you know."

"How?" It was a whisper.

His eyes seemed to probe her mind, her heart. "I'll have

to trust you. I made another telephone call tonight. Later I got my instructions."

"Your doctor?"

"My—oh, that was an excuse. There is nothing wrong with me physically. I simply need a reason for holing up in Simonton for a while, but now your brother's condition can supply that reason more plausibly." He added coldly but with deadly conviction, "If you ever betray me to anyone, for any reason, you'll wish you had never been born."

"But I don't understand." She was bewildered. The day had brought so many shocks that she felt as though she were being whirled around and around by a tornado. "I don't understand."

"The man I talked to," he said deliberately, "was my boss. I explained—about Cynthia; about you." There was no expression on his face but Nancy's cheeks burned. "There are to be no changes in my plans. Except, of course, that I can't be married tomorrow as I had intended."

Unconsciously his finger traced the line of the scratch on his cheek. "It takes three days in New York to go through the formalities. My present marriage license is no longer—useful. But after that we'll go to Simonton." Seeing her trapped expression he grinned mirthlessly. "Your brother will be along for your protection," he reminded her. "So far as anyone in the village is to know, you are the girl I originally planned to marry. Fortunately, I never mentioned Cynthia's name. She wanted to keep our marriage private. Those are your instructions."

He sounded, the girl thought stormily, like a tough sergeant snapping orders at the troops.

He went on, "My plans for the diplomatic service have been temporarily disrupted by your brother's illness. Please remember that. We will stay in Simonton until he recuperates. I will devote myself to painting. You will be free to do as you choose with your time so long as you confide in no one. But be careful not to let yourself be trapped into any impulsive admissions. You're rather an impulsive girl, you know. Is that clear?"

For a long time she was silent.

"It was originally your idea," he reminded her mockingly.

"I know, but I thought—only an engagement. A pretend engagement. I didn't expect to marry anyone."

"Don't let the idea of marriage bother you. I count on you not to damage my name. We've kept it clean and honorable for generations. Beyond that—we needn't pretend we are interested in each other, need we, except when we are with other people. Each of us is quite honestly making use of the other's needs to serve his own purpose. I won't—bother you. Never again will I look on any woman as my wife. All that died today."

After a pause he asked, "Agreed?"

"Agreed," she said, and they shook hands gravely.

II

In front of the shabby building in which she had rented a furnished room he asked in some surprise, "Have you been comfortable here?"

She shrugged. "It's close to the hospital, easy walking distance, and I couldn't afford anything better. My brother has always paid my expenses and given me an allowance, but that is nearly gone now and I didn't like to bother him, especially when he can't earn anything himself and his medical and surgical expenses must be terrific. All that plastic surgery. And more to come, of course."

Before getting out of the warm car she started to fasten her coat, gave a little exclamation of annoyance and bent over to search the floor of the car. The top button of her dress had fallen off. The dress opened at the neck and as Peter switched on the overhead lights to look for the button he caught sight of the pearl necklace she was wearing, concealed under the plain wool dress.

"In the morning, then," he said as he walked to the door of the building with her. "We'll see your brother and then start the machinery of getting a marriage license. Good night, Nancy."

"Good night—Peter." She went into the dim hallway and out of sight, walking confidently, head high. But when the door of her room had closed behind her, she sagged against it. What am I getting into, she thought frantically. Something was wrong.

Back in the big Rolls Peter closed his eyes. What was he getting into? Something was wrong. The girl seemed to be short of money and yet she wore a necklace of matched pearls hidden under her dress. Dr. Warburton, while he had confirmed her story, had done so only after considerable persuasion and with evident reluctance. There was something he knew about his patient, Noah Jones, which he had no intention of revealing. In fact, Peter had had a great deal of difficulty in convincing the doctor that he was not an eager reporter for a newspaper or a legman for a television network.

For some reason Noah Jones had been careful to keep his sister out of his country, out of his life. Why?

Peter shrugged. Sooner or later he would find out. Not that it mattered particularly, unless the Joneses were involved in a scandal or something criminal. That would put a period to his diplomatic career. But even that, at the moment, was of no particular importance. The bottom had dropped out of his world.

Cynthia! At last he let the thought of her pervade his mind. He surrendered helplessly to the pain.

FIVE

"I, PETER, take you, Anne, to be my wedded wife."

In the dim quiet of the church Nancy stood as though in a dream. Multicolored light pouring through a stained glass window made her seem curiously unreal. Like a mosaic. Like one of the figures on the glass itself, head bowed, great dark eyes wide, looking almost blind, the beautifully curved lips colorless.

Peter's voice, resonant and assured, startled her in the quiet. She felt the ring slide over her finger, heard the clergyman say, a smile in his voice, "You may kiss your bride, Mr. Gerard."

She braced herself but Peter's light, impersonal kiss barely touched her lips.

"I wish you every happiness, Mrs. Gerard," the clergyman said.

Mrs. Gerard! Nancy Jones was gone forever. This was Anne Gerard, facing the unknown with terror in her heart, turmoil in her brain, a gallant smile on her lips. The clergyman was speaking to her. She began to comprehend the words.

"In this new united life you begin together . . ."

United! Surely no two people could be so divided, so separate, so unknown to each other.

"Remember," the clergyman was saying, "that marriage is a profession like any other business of living. Trust your husband and love him."

Trust. That was all Peter had asked of her. If she only

knew—but there was some secret she must not be told. Something lay hidden behind the door of Bluebeard's chamber which she had been forbidden to open.

"Marriage, of course," the clergyman was saying when she heeded his words again, "is a key to many doors."

Bluebeard's door, Nancy thought.

"That key may lead to a sympathetic comradeship which increases in sweetness and strength and understanding as the years pass; it may lead to the pitfalls of intolerance and irritability. A united life, Peter and Anne. A patient and long understanding of each other's convictions and tastes and temperaments. The ability to bend a little, to give up a little. Sometimes I think it is only the small things that count, that disrupt a marriage, the momentary and trivial irritations. The same key fits many doors. Some may open on joy and some on sorrow. You can encounter either confidently if you love each other enough and keep locked the doors of doubt and distrust."

Doubt and distrust. Behind his unrevealing face Peter was sardonically amused. About the only feelings he had toward the girl at his side were those of doubt and distrust.

"Whatever comes, in the years ahead, I trust that the relationship between you will grow and deepen, that you will become most truly one person. May God bless you both."

Then the witnesses supplied by the clergyman signed the register and Peter took Nancy's arm to lead her down the aisle, past the empty pews, to the street. The clergyman's troubled eyes followed them. He had known Peter Gerard all his life, had known his father, had known of his grandfather, the formidable and forbidding old Simon Gerard who had skyrocketed a million dollars into a great fortune. He had always assumed that when the young man married, the church would be filled with wedding guests, bright and fragrant with flowers, that a red carpet would be unrolled from the entrance to the curb, that reporters and photographers would record the arrival and departure of the bride and groom. There had, he felt, been no happiness in the two young faces. Before the altar he knelt to pray for the couple he had just married.

I

Max put down his book—today he was reading contemporary history—and opened the door of the Rolls.

"Max," Peter told him, "this is Mrs. Gerard. We were just married."

Max beamed. "That is good news, sir. Best wishes to you both."

Nancy smiled at him. "Thank you, Max."

When Peter had given the address of the hospital and stepped in beside her, he said matter-of-factly, as though he had been selecting neckties rather than getting married, "There's one thing, Nancy; your brother is no fool. We've got to put on a better act for him. He figured something was wrong when I met him the other day."

He remembered the meeting clearly. Before entering Noah's room, Nancy had warned him not to reveal any shock when he saw her brother's disfigurement. He had, he thought, succeeded, though he had not anticipated the extent of the scars that seamed the man's face. He had not been prepared, either, for the skeleton-thin hand that had clasped his. Above all, he had not expected the alert intelligence in the eyes that summed him up, or the barrage of questions that Noah had fired at him.

How had he met Nancy? How long had he known her? How long had they been engaged? How did he plan to take care of her?

Peter, who had, with Nancy's help, prepared his answers in advance, had been somewhat amused.

Unexpectedly, Noah had grinned at him. "After all, I'm the only family the girl has, Gerard. I just want to be sure she's in good hands."

"You can count on me. I'll take care of her. And my name is Peter."

"Welcome to the family, Peter."

"Thank you, Noah."

The interview had seemed to go all right but Peter was aware that, before he and Nancy left, Noah was beginning to watch their expressions. He obviously sensed that something was wrong.

He had refused to attend the wedding ceremony. "I don't go out," he said shortly. "I don't see people. With this mug—" He dropped the subject.

It was only when Peter had explained about the guest-house and had assured Noah that he could be completely alone that he agreed to go up to Connecticut with them.

"Though it seems damned odd to me that you want a third on a honeymoon," he commented.

Peter smiled at him. "You won't be a third. We won't know you are around."

So far as a male attendant was concerned, Noah flatly refused, with the unreason of a sick man, though he was obviously unable to look after himself.

It was Nancy who provided a solution. "It seems hardly fair that Max should have to give up his classes to spend the winter in Connecticut."

"Actually, after two years at it, he abandoned his night courses. Since then he has been trying to supplement his education by wide reading; the best way, after all, to get an education. But, of course, he needs some guidance."

"There's a job for you, Noah," Nancy had said gaily. "Help Max pick out books, talk to him about them. He deserves a break. And, in return, he could lend you a hand when you need it."

"That's an idea," Noah had admitted.

The Rolls drew up at the entrance to the hospital. Nancy waited in the car while Peter and Max went inside to get Noah. The day was bitterly cold, though the interior of the car was warm. Nervously Nancy pulled off her glove, looked at the thin platinum band of her wedding ring. She was married! In a few minutes she would be driving to a strange place with a strange man. And she was his wife. She fought down panic. This was no time to worry about herself. Peter had been right. Noah had found something puzzling about their relationship. For his sake, she must act convincingly the part of a happy bride.

The hospital doors opened, Max came out to open the door of the car; Peter followed, pushing a small wheel-chair in which Noah sat, fully clothed for the first time since his accident, bundled into a heavy overcoat, a scarf covering his chin, a hat pulled down over the eyes that were concealed behind dark glasses.

As the brilliant light struck him, he instinctively flung up a hand to conceal his scarred face. Then, with the help of the two men, he was lifted into the back seat beside Nancy. Peter followed, while Max folded the chair and stowed it in the trunk of the car.

"Here we are, darling," Peter said cheerfully. "Noah was ready, he had already checked out at the desk, and now we are off."

Noah turned to scrutinize his sister's face. "Well, Mrs. Gerard!" He bent over to kiss her check. "No one forbade the banns?"

She held out her hand with its wedding ring. "Everything's wonderful," she declared. "Everything's marvelous. Everything's—"

"Okay, I get the picture." Noah turned to Peter. "Now if you can just keep her thinking that—"

"I'll do my best, Noah."

Noah leaned back in the car, tired from the unaccustomed exertion of dressing, upset at leaving behind him the solitude and security of the familiar hospital room. Then he sat up.

"You must want to choke me! A third on a honeymoon."

"You won't be," Peter said in an odd tone.

Nancy, seeing her brother's narrowed eyes, his quick look of speculation, of suspicion, said gaily, "Peter, we're just going off into the blue, so far as I am concerned. What with all the excitement, and one thing and another, I've never really learned anything about your home."

"Your home now," he reminded her, picking up her cue quickly. "You'll both see it for yourselves in a couple of hours so I don't dare build it up too much. Simonton is a village of five thousand people in northwest Connecticut. It was named for my great-grandfather, who, to judge by his pictures, was a grim old boy. Simonton has no industry on a large scale, no factories. Actually, the biggest business the place has, believe it or not, is the sale of harpsichords, spinets, lutes, recorders, and replicas of other ancient instruments. There is no railroad."

He was silent for a moment, considering. "It's not in a sense what's called a 'quaint' New England village, but I think it's beautiful. In May, there's a display of lilacs that's out of this world. In October, the autumn colors stop your heart. When there's a heavy snow or an ice storm, it's like a postcard view. After the leaves fall, there's a view of rolling blue hills."

Peter broke off as he saw his new brother-in-law smiling. "I'm afraid I sound like a real estate prospectus," he said apologetically.

"You really love the place, don't you? Then why do you spend so much of your time abroad?"

Peter's diplomatic duties had already been used to explain his meeting with Nancy in Europe.

Peter hesitated, took his time lighting his pipe. "There's nothing I would rather do than stay at home. I don't," he said slowly, "know any way of explaining myself without sounding like a pompous ass. It's—well, there's too much money in my family. There ought to be some—return— some—"

Noah laughed. "You feel as guilty at admitting to a conscience as most men would at being discovered committing a crime."

Peter laughed with him.

"Just the same," Nancy put in, "I'm not sure you are right about this, Peter."

He turned almost as though he had forgotten her presence.

"Why? Don't you like the idea of being a diplomat's wife?" There was bitterness in his voice now.

He is thinking of Cynthia, Nancy realized. He is remembering that she wanted to be a diplomat's wife. Unexpectedly, it was his pain that troubled her, that she wanted to ease.

"Diplomat or not, what does it matter? I'm your wife and I'm with you all the way, whatever you want to do. But you have so much—it seems to me, Peter, that a man with talent like yours has something special, important, to give the world. Something unique. You have no right to waste that talent."

"What's all this talent?" Noah demanded.

"He can paint, Noah! How he can paint! He could be one of the truly great ones."

Her enthusiasm and faith were so genuine that the doubt faded from Noah's eyes. "What are you doing, Peter? Hiding your light under a bushel?"

"Well, I'll give it a chance to glow this winter." Peter grinned. "I'll really buckle down to work. After that, we'll see."

"We'll see," Nancy said confidently.

"Look out for this girl, Peter," Noah warned him. "I didn't say anything before you were married because I didn't want to discourage you, but she's a born crusader with an exasperating touch of Florence Nightingale. I can see right now that she is going to keep your nose to the grindstone. You'll be slaving away like a dog."

"That bad?"

"Worse. And while I'm giving you this brotherly advice, when she gets an idea, you had better head for the tall timber. A dangerous woman, that's my Nancy." He corrected himself. "Our Nancy."

"My Nancy," Peter said.

At his request the car made a sharp right turn onto a steep little side road, then rolled through a long red covered bridge. Beyond the bridge Max parked where they could look at the famous old structure, the water beneath it seeming black in contrast with the patches of ice and snow on the banks.

"All right," Peter said, "we can go on. I just wanted you to get a picture of an authentic piece of old New England."

The car turned, went back through the covered bridge. Then it swept smoothly and effortlessly up a long hill, Max's hands steady on the wheel, his eyes alert for treacherous patches of ice. It was much colder here in the hills, though they were little more than a hundred miles from New York City.

The Rolls stopped at a blinker, turned left along an unexpectedly broad avenue. This was not a typical New England village green with white houses and a soaring church spire. On either side, the houses were spacious, with ample grounds.

They followed a high stone wall, turned between open iron gates, and along a driveway that ended in a circular sweep in front of a long Palladian house of gray field-stone. Here and there on the grounds great elms and maples stood stark against the sky. In the distance, to the north, behind the house, were the curving lines of blue hills.

Max opened the folding chair and he and Peter helped Noah into it.

"The guesthouse is around at the back," Peter said, seeing Noah's hands clench at the thought of facing people. "Max will take you there and see you get settled." He added casually, "He has a room upstairs. All you have to do is call. As the Spaniards say, 'You are in your house.'"

"Thank you, Peter. Nancy—"

She bent to kiss his cheek. "See you tomorrow," she said gaily.

The front door opened and a middle-aged woman with graying hair appeared at the entrance.

"That's Mrs. Henning, the housekeeper," Peter said in a low tone. He raised his voice. "Don't come out in the cold, Mrs. Henning." He gathered a startled Nancy up in his arms, carried her up the broad, shallow steps, through the doorway, laughing. He kissed her deliberately, slowly, on the lips.

"Welcome home, Mrs. Gerard," he said and set her on her feet.

The surprised protest was checked on her lips when she saw the servants clustered in the hallway to welcome her. They were smiling broadly. Peter, she was beginning to realize, was a fast man with an idea.

"This is my wife," he said, and introduced them, one at a time, to Nancy.

She smiled, shook hands, had a pleasant word for each of them.

She's a thoroughbred, Peter thought in relief. I believe we're going to get away with this thing.

He said aloud, "Are Mrs. Gerard's rooms ready?"

"Quite ready, sir," Mrs. Henning said. "After you tele-phoned, I was able to get a maid to look after madam.

Just sheer luck. She came to the door, looking for work. She hasn't any training, but if madam can manage for a while and the girl doesn't prove satisfactory, I'll get someone else from our regular New York employment agency."

For a little while, after the servants had withdrawn to their duties, Nancy stood looking around her. A house in a New England village. She hadn't anticipated anything like this. An old homestead, maybe. A Cape Cod cottage, perhaps. At most, a spacious Colonial building. Her heart sank. She would never be able to cope with her duties as hostess in an establishment on this scale.

The housekeeper said, "Perhaps you'd like me to show you around before you go to your rooms, madam. Unless —"She looked inquiringly at Peter who had handed his hat, coat, and gloves to the butler.

"That's a sound idea," he said absently. "I'll check to see that Mr. Jones is comfortable. The guesthouse has been prepared for my brother-in-law, hasn't it?"

"Oh, yes, sir. Everything is ready, the bed made up, a fire in the fireplace. We had an electric bell installed so he can reach Max whenever he needs him."

"Fine!" With a nod to Nancy, Peter went out of doors.

Mrs. Henning shook her head. "No coat, and the temperature nearly zero. Some day he'll catch his death of cold. His poor mother would have had a fit. Well—"

The hallway was long and wide, with a gracious staircase that branched halfway up, and a balcony above that overlooked it.

On the right there was a large and unexpectedly formal drawing room. Behind that was a library, the walls booklined, with comfortable chairs and good reading lamps. Beyond that was a smaller room, informal, with lighter colors and a kind of gaiety about it. There were low tables and plants and a fire that crackled, its flames reflecting on white tiles.

"What a dear room!" Nancy exclaimed.

"This was Mrs. Gerard's morning room. She used it for answering mail and making out menus and seeing her own friends. She kept her appointment book here, too. It wasn't used a great deal as her sitting room is upstairs."

"I wish I could have known her," Nancy said softly.

"A lovely lady. A very lovely lady." The housekeeper started on but Nancy had paused to look at a landscape on the wall. The painter had chosen as his subject a small area of the grounds of this house at the fleeting moment when winter is withdrawing reluctantly, when spring is arriving hesitantly. The least lovely season of the year. The snow has gone, no green has yet appeared; there is desolation and yet a mysterious stirring. Something tremendous is about to happen.

"It's marvelous," Nancy said in a low voice. She added confidently, "Peter painted that."

The housekeeper nodded. "Yes, that's Mr. Gerard's work. His mother loved it." She hesitated. "I don't understand art. I can't help wondering why he didn't choose something prettier. You should see our roses, madam. They are famous."

It occurred to Nancy that she would not be here to see the famous roses. Long before they bloomed, Noah would have recovered sufficiently to be on his own and Peter would have accomplished whatever mysterious thing he had come here to do.

She was silent as the housekeeper led the way back to the big hallway and into the huge state dining room that took up most of the other side of the main floor. Beyond that there was, she discovered in relief, a smaller, more informal dining room. The rest of the main floor consisted of a kitchen, pantries, and servants' dining room.

The second floor was bisected by a corridor, a deep red carpet on the floor, five doors on either side. Mrs. Henning led the way to the last door on the right.

"These were Mrs. Gerard's rooms. Of course, you'll want to make changes, but we left them just as they were."

There was a small suite of rooms. The little sitting room, like the other rooms which Peter's mother had occupied, had a quality of gaiety. Beyond, with a lovely view over distant hills, was the bedroom, bright and cheerful. Off it was an unexpectedly luxurious bathroom.

The grounds, Nancy saw, were much more extensive than she had realized. There were flowerbeds, a great sweep of lawn, tremendous ancient trees, the little guest-house, and at the back the ground sloped steeply down into a valley.

"Thank you, Mrs. Henning." Nancy dismissed the housekeeper with a smile. "I'll see the rest of the house tomorrow." She added inpulsively, "I'm so glad you're here! I have no experience at running a household."

The older woman smiled back. "We're glad you're here, too, madam. Mr. Gerard being so artistic and all, we always hoped he'd have a beautiful wife. And perhaps he will be here more often. It's been lonely for him since his mother died. He—we all think a lot of him. Perhaps you'd like to rest for a while. Dinner is usually served at seven-thirty, unless you'd rather change the time."

"That will be fine," Nancy said vaguely.

For a long time she wandered back and forth in the charming suite of rooms that had belonged to Peter's mother. She felt like an intruder here.

Once more she returned to the bedroom to look at the view, but the early winter darkness had swallowed it up. There was nothing to see but long oblongs of light. Of course, those were the windows in the guesthouse. As she looked, the door opened and Peter stood silhouetted against the light.

"Good night, Noah!" he called cheerfully. "If Max doesn't look out for you properly—"

In the background she heard Noah's resonant, carrying voice. "Look after me! He thinks he's a damned nurse-maid. First thing I know, he'll be feeding me with a spoon."

Peter laughed and the door of the guesthouse closed. Then there was only darkness. No, there were patches of light on the grounds, probably from the kitchen where dinner would be in preparation.

The front door opened and closed. Footsteps could be heard on the great staircase. They were coming down the corridor. Nancy, her heart thudding, ran out of the bedroom into the little sitting room. She discovered that she was shaking and she sat down, hiding her trembling hands behind her.

There was a tap at the door. She steadied her voice. "Come in," she called.

Peter opened the door, looked swiftly around without entering the room. "Everything all right? Will you be comfortable?"

"It's wonderful." She regretted the warmth and enthusiasm in her voice, fearing that he might misunderstand it. He didn't.

"Good. Alter anything you like, of course. Just tell Mrs. Henning what you want. If you are nervous—strange house and all that, and, of course, it's not Manhattan; there's not a light to be seen at night—ring the bell beside your bed or give me a shout. My rooms are just across the hall."

"Th—thank you."

"We usually dress for dinner. Mother liked a little formality. But if you'd rather not—"

"I bought a dinner dress yesterday."

"All right." He added impersonally, "That reminds me, I've set up checking accounts for you and arranged charge accounts in New York so you can get whatever you need."

"I don't—" she began

"As my wife you'll need to meet people, do a fair amount of entertaining." His mouth twisted wryly. "You're supposed to be a bride and with the normally adequate trousseau. You'll have to think of some convincing story—you're rather good at that—to account for coming here without much luggage."

"I—all right."

"There's nothing to be afraid of," he said irritably. "Nothing at all. If you think for a moment I'll forget what your position here really is, you're a very stupid girl."

"Why—why—why—" She stuttered in her fury.

"Dinner's at half-past seven," he said, ignoring her rage. "You've had a rough week. Tonight you can get to bed early and catch up on some rest."

The door of her sitting room closed behind him. A moment later she heard a second door open and close. There was an air of finality about it.

SIX

THE MAID who had been assigned to Nancy—"I am Ferrell, madam"—was tall for a girl and much too thin. She had a slight stoop as though she were trying to conceal her height. Watching her in the mirror, seeing the sensitive features—too sensitive, too vulnerable—Nancy realized that the girl was frightened and desperately shy. She wore no makeup, her brown hair was cut plainly and uncurled. Her eyes—but the heavy yellow glasses she wore hid her eyes.

"What's your first name?" Nancy asked in her beautiful warm voice.

"Helen, madam."

Nancy smiled at her. "I like Helen better."

The maid lifted the dress carefully over Nancy's head, watched it fall in long folds to the floor. It was a gold sheath of heavy satin out of which Nancy's gleaming shoulders and arms emerged. Tonight, in the formal gold evening dress that set off her black hair and eyes and brilliant mouth, she surveyed herself thoughtfully. *Like a zombie,* she remembered.

"Madam is beautiful," the maid exclaimed, and then blushed.

Nancy looked at herself in some surprise. Beautiful? It didn't seem possible.

"And that gorgeous dress," the maid breathed.

"Thank heaven, there are still some dressmakers who

51

make clothes for women who want to look like women, not clothes that look as though a girl was preparing to play tennis!" Nancy exclaimed.

There was a tap on the sitting room door and Helen went to answer it. A murmur of voices. When she returned to the bedroom she held out a jewel case.

"Mr. Gerard said—the groom's gift to the bride. He hopes you will wear it tonight."

Nancy opened the case and they both cried out. Slowly Nancy lifted out the diamond necklace, staring at it almost in disbelief. Then she thought, of course, he bought it for Cynthia.

She started to put it back in the jewel case. Hesitated. He had asked her to wear it. She would return it, of course, when this farce of a marriage was over, but now she must do as he asked.

Helen fastened the glittering necklace around Nancy's white throat with cold, shaking fingers. Together they looked in the mirror at the incredible jewels.

"It's madness to keep a thing like this up here in the country," Nancy said at last. "Tomorrow it must go to a bank the very first thing."

She became aware that, behind those thick-lensed glasses, Helen was watching her in surprise. She had expressed no word of pleasure or of gratitude for this fabulous gift.

"I shan't need you again tonight, Helen."

The maid gave her a quick nod of comprehension. "Good night, madam."

Nancy felt her cheeks flushing. Of course. This was her bridal night. *A very stupid girl,* her loving bridegroom had called her. She went slowly along the corridor, more slowly down the great staircase.

"Mr. Gerard is in the library, madam," the butler said. He had come into the great hall so quietly that Nancy had not been aware of his approach. Unlike the butler at the New York house, this one was elderly, thin, imperturbable.

She nodded and went into the library. Peter was standing at the mantel, looking moodily into the fire. In his dinner jacket he seemed more imposing, more remote, or perhaps she felt that because he was now the unknown quantity, her husband. *A very stupid girl.* For a long moment she watched him, unobserved. The face that had been so mocking, so contemptuous when she had last seen him was only unhappy. And very lonely.

Above the mantel there was a portrait which bore a striking resemblance to the man who stood looking into the fire. The same heavy dark hair, the same broad sweep of forehead, the same deep-socketed eyes, the same mouth and firm jaw. But it was not, of course, a portrait of Peter Gerard. The high stock at the neck, the heavily embroidered dark velvet coat belonged to a period of more than a hundred and fifty years earlier.

As though aware of her silent scrutiny Peter turned quickly, the mask back on his face. He looked at her in the gold evening dress and caught his breath. After a moment, as though he had sustained a shock of some kind, he said, almost breathlessly, "Thank you for wearing the necklace."

"Thank you for letting me wear it. I've never seen anything so magnificent. But, Peter, isn't it a bit—much— for a quiet dinner for two in the country? I'm terrified something will happen to it."

"After dinner I'll put it in the safe, if you like."

"I do like."

"But Murch—"

"That's the butler?"

"Yes. He's been with the Gerards for fifty years in one capacity or another. He'd smell a rat if my bride didn't have any jewelry."

"Oh."

There were voices in the hallway, Murch quiet but insistent. "I'm sorry, sir, but Mr. Gerard is not at home."

"Of course he's home!" The answering voice was gay and confident. "Out of the way, Murch, and stop making silly noises." The voice was raised to call, "Hey, Peter!"

Peter laughed. "That's Dick Stowell, the best friend I have in the world." He went to the door. "All right, Murch, call off the dogs and let the man in."

"I *am* in," Stowell said triumphantly.

"And—another place for dinner. Hello, Dick!"

"What's all this mystery? 'Mr. Gerard is not at home.' I saw the car earlier this afternoon with these old eyes. Well, Peter, it's good to have you back. Staying long?"

"All winter, perhaps."

"All—" There was a pause. "But, good lord, man! I thought that diplomatic post was in the bag. If the government boys have been giving you the run-around I'm going to clobber them personally. They don't know a good man when they see him."

"Cool off!" Peter laughed. His voice dropped. Nancy heard fragments of speech. ". . . married . . . my wife's brother . . . complete seclusion while he recovers." Then he raised his voice. "Come along and meet my wife, Dick."

The two men entered the library. Stowell was a big man, a good two inches over six feet, with the shoulders of a football player, and a broad, beaming, outdoor sort of face. A cheerful extrovert, Nancy thought. He wasn't handsome but he had an attractive, impudent sort of personality.

As he caught sight of her, his face reflected something of the shock Nancy had seen in Peter's when she had entered the room in her long gold dress.

"This," Peter said, his voice reflecting his pleasure in seeing his old friend, "is Richard Stowell. Dick, my wife. Nancy," he went on lightly, "you might as well get reconciled to this guy. He's known as the pest around the house. No getting rid of him. He has poor Murch terrorized."

Dick Stowell crushed Nancy's hand in his. "Not a syllable of truth in it," he declared. "My meekness is a legend. Children learn about it at their mother's knee." He turned to Peter. "She's beautiful! How did you manage to capture a girl like this?"

His eyes were caught by the spectacular diamond necklace. When he looked into Nancy's eyes again it was with a question and less friendliness. He thinks I married Peter for his money, Nancy realized. She felt her quick temper rising. But at least he cares about Peter's happiness, she thought, about the kind of girl who marries him.

Impulsively she said, "Please try to like me, Mr. Stowell. For Peter's sake."

Peter gave her a look of sardonic amusement but his friend beamed. "That's going to be the easiest job I ever did. And nice people call me Dick."

She laughed. "All right, Dick."

Murch appeared in the doorway. "A telephone call Mr. Gerard."

"My instructions were that I am not at home tonight."

"It's Washington calling, sir."

Peter excused himself and went out. Nancy settled in a chair near the fire, a chair that was much too big for her slender figure. Dick Stowell, one shoulder braced against the mantel, looked down at her. The friendly smile had gone.

Peter told me about your brother, that he's the reason you two are planning to stay in Simonton for a while."

Nancy nodded without speaking.

Stowell cleared his throat, drummed his fingers on the mantel. He was embarrassed but he went ahead doggedly anyhow. "We're old friends, Peter and I. They don't come any better than Peter." He cleared his throat again. "He's all set for an important career, you know. His big chance is coming up in a few weeks' time."

"I know."

"I suppose your brother—there was no other solution for him?"

"There really wasn't," Nancy told him. "It has to be like this. I'm sorry, too, Mr.—Dick. But, after all, Peter is merely postponing his displomatic career, not abandoning it altogether."

"I hope so. What happened to your brother?"

"A motor accident. His wife was killed. Noah was badly hurt and—horribly disfigured. That's why he won't see people. And his will to live seemed to go."

"Too bad."

Stowell did not seem unduly sympathetic. He looked, Nancy thought, like a man who had never had a day's illness in his life. He couldn't possibly understand anyone like Noah.

Nancy felt trapped. She had agreed to this fantastic

arrangement. Agreed? She had asked for it, hadn't she? And she had done it for Noah's sake. Now, unexpectedly, Noah was being blamed for the sacrifice of Peter's career. It wasn't true, of course. Peter had made that sacrifice for personal reasons. And she couldn't explain, couldn't justify herself, to Dick Stowell, even though he was Peter's best friend. If any explaining was to be done, Peter would have to do it himself.

After Peter returned, making no comment about his telephone call, the butler announced dinner, which was served in the smaller of the two dining rooms. The service was flawless, the food superlative, but Nancy, pushing it about on her plate, almost untasted, was scarcely aware of her surroundings. Once she looked up to find Dick Stowell staring at her.

"What gets me, Peter," he said, "is that I'd have sworn your fiancée was a blonde. I remember that painting you did of her."

"Oh, that," Peter said easily, "was just a model I used for a while. Good models are hard to find. Either they aren't the right type or they can't hold a pose, or they jabber. I'm going to get a lot of painting done this winter, I hope." Resolutely he shifted the conversation away from Cynthia to general problems of painting.

"You seem to have your work cut out for you," Stowell commented. "But how about your beautiful bride? Is she going to live in splendid isolation in Simonton like her brother?"

For a moment Peter was at a loss. It was Nancy who said quickly, "Tell me what the village people are like, Dick, and what they are going to expect of me."

"Caesar's wife," he told her bluntly.

"Oh, dear," she said in dismay.

"You haven't grasped yet what people think of the Gerards. So far as Simonton is concerned, the Gerards are the star on the Christmas tree, the guardian angels, the social arbiters."

"Oh, don't overdo it!" Peter exclaimed, half amused, half annoyed.

"I'm not. I just want to put Nancy in the picture. To fortify her."

"You've terrified me," she admitted. "But tell me about them."

"They are nice people, on the whole. Of course, during the winter there's practically no social life, if that's any consolation to you, so you can ease into the situation. The retired and the well-heeled—far more than you would find in most villages of this size—spend their winters in Arizona or California, on the Riviera or in Egypt. They follow the sun. And a very nice program it is for them as can afford it. A few old families like the Gerards, who put down their roots here in pre-revolutionary days. As I said, some well-heeled retired people. A few artists, who are not so well-heeled. And me, of course. I'm the town's chief liability."

"That's his backhanded way of showing off, Nancy," Peter put in. "Dick writes science fiction and he's awfully good at it."

"A hack, that's what I am. An outcast from the finer things of life."

Nancy laughed. "I don't believe a word of it. I'm going to start reading your books."

"Heaven help you."

"But tell me, what do people do here in the winter?"

"Hibernate."

"Oh, look here, Peter protested, "you'll be giving her the wrong idea."

"If you want the lowdown on the village, Nancy," Dick said, "you ought to see Joe Hacker. In fact, willy-nilly, you are going to see Joe Hacker. As soon as he gets wind of this marriage, he'll beat a path to the door for an interview."

Seeing her bewildered look, Peter explained, "Hacker used to be a New York newspaper man. Now he is the owner, editor, and practically the entire staff of the Simonton *Weekly Gazette*. From what I've seen of him he's a nice chap, above the job he has but it seems to satisfy something in him. Perhaps the pace of Manhattan was too much for him."

"You know, Peter," Dick said thoughtfully, "I'm not so sure you are right about that. Hacker isn't the usual small-town newspaper man. Not by a long shot. He was a

Pulitzer Prize winner at one time. What's he doing here? He's always trying to ferret out information. Come on him suddenly and he starts like a startled fawn. And what does he do all week in that little printing plant of his? Something darned queer there, if you ask me."

It was nearly eleven when Dick took his leave with a cheerful, "Brace yourself, lady. You're going to see a lot of me."

When he had gone there was a long silence in the library, which Nancy broke at length.

"I'm sorry, Peter, that your friend doesn't like me. I seem to have failed the first test."

Peter's brows rose in surprise. "I got the impression that you bowled him over."

She shook her head. "That was just his loyalty to you. While you were on the telephone before dinner he made it pretty clear that he thought I had damaged your career by foisting Noah on you and keeping you pinned down in Simonton. He seems to think that there could have been some other solution."

When Peter made no reply she got up, removed the necklace, and held it out to him.

"Please take care of it."

He took it from her, dropped it in the pocket of his dinner jacket. "I'll put in the safe tonight." He glanced at his watch. "I'll have to make a long-distance call."

She nodded without speaking and started for the door.

"What's wrong, Nancy?"

She turned to face him. "I don't know," she admitted. "A kind of foreboding. Like Juliet perhaps: 'I have no joy in this contract tonight; it is too rash, too ill-advised, too sudden.' "

He shrugged. "Well, we can't turn back now. The die is cast. Good night."

"Good night." She went up the stairs, her long skirt whispering over the steps, one slim hand on the railing. She did not look back.

I

Peter called the emergency number he had been given. His call was answered on the first ring.

"I'd like all the background stuff you can get on Joe Hacker. H-a-c-k-e-r ... That's right. Former New York newspaper man. Once a Pulitzer Prize winner. Now owner and editor of the Simonton *Weekly Gazette* ... No special reason. His name cropped up tonight in rather an odd way ... Well, yes, there's one more thing ... No, just clearing as I go."

When he had finished the call, Peter went into the formal dining room, knelt beside the long table, his fingers groping. He slid aside what appeared to be a piece of carving on the lower part of the table, dialed a combination, and the door of the small safe slid open. He placed the necklace inside, closed the safe, and went upstairs, walking as though he were very tired.

He did not glance at the door of Nancy's suite. He opened his own door across the hall and closed it quietly behind him. The front room, corresponding to Nancy's sitting room, was his bedroom. The room at the back of the house, corresponding to her bedroom, was a studio. The whole wall and part of the ceiling had been converted into a large window, whose light could be controlled by a complicated series of draw curtains. It was an unexpectedly functional room. Except for one chair, an easel, and a table cluttered with tubes of paints and brushes there was no furniture. Canvases were hung on the walls or stacked on the floor.

On the easel was the portrait he had done of Cynthia. For a long time Peter stood looking at it, his face somber. How lovely she had seemed! How sweet. How deeply he had loved her.

No, he realized bitterly, what he had loved was the girl he had imagined her to be. The eyes, as soft as pansies in the painting, had become as cold as steel. The gentle, almost childish voice, had grown shrill and vulgar.

Crawl back, she had said. *Crawl back.* Anger licked

along his veins. *Not my type.* And he had said, in his disillusionment and bitterness, that he would prefer to marry the first girl he met.

Well, that was what he had done. More fool he. But after that telephone call he had made, while Nancy slept in the New York house, he had received specific instructions.

They were sorry, Brooks had told him, to complicate matters for him, but on the whole they were delighted with the situation which had developed. Brooks expressed perfunctory regret over Peter's broken engagement, but this Jones girl with her fantastic proposal would be ideal. Better to have a truly and demonstrably sick man on the scene than to have any faked symptoms of Peter's. He was to go ahead with the marriage.

Peter had listened, pinching his lower lip between his fingers.

"Any further questions?" Brooks had asked.

"Yes, sir. You've got something up your sleeve. I'd like a look at it."

"Something rather unexpected cropped up. May not be important. In any case, the Fourteenth Street place was staked out. I don't know how they got on to it. The problem is that you may have been seen when you arrived or when you left. If they are on to you, it means that you'll have to watch your step. Try to throw them off the track if you possibly can."

"I—see."

"Take care of yourself," Brooks said cheerfully, and broke the connection.

SEVEN

AND THAT, Peter thought savagely, was the end of a perfect day. He had contracted a loveless marriage, a mock marriage, to provide a convincing reason for his presence in Simonton; and his cover, if Brooks had guessed correctly, was suspect before he had even tackled his job.

He had lost the girl he wanted and married one he didn't want. Nonetheless, her unexpected beauty, when she had walked into the library in her gold dress, had jolted him. Not a madonna; A Delilah who was not aware of her own enchantment. Beauty like that could easily create a complication. Peter made up his mind that it would not. He and Nancy would keep up appearances for the world. Beyond that, they would go their separate ways.

As he came up the stairs, he had heard the sound of a key being turned in the lock of Nancy's door. He smiled grimly. She needn't worry. A key. A key? What did that remind him of? Of course, the clergyman's words that morning. Marriage, he had said, was a key to many doors. Well, there was one door for which Peter would never want a key, the door behind which his wife had needlessly locked herself.

His wife! There was a lot he would like to know about Nancy Jones. Nancy Gerard, he reminded himself wryly. He would like to know why her brother had been so anxious to keep her out of his life. He would like to know how she had got possession of that valuable pearl necklace which she had worn, carefully hidden under her dress.

He wasn't alone in his distrust. Dick, for all his obvious admiration of her beauty, had not been happy about the marriage. He had resented the fact that Nancy's brother should prove an obstacle to his career.

Peter smiled to himself, warmed by his sense of Dick's fine loyalty, but uncomfortably aware that Noah was being blamed unjustly for his presence in Simonton, his abandonment, temporarily, at least, of his career. Just the same, Peter intended to take full advantage of Noah's illness and, if it should prove necessary, to override his reluctance to see people.

Peter shrugged and rubbed his head, which was beginning to pound. He'd better get some aspirin. His headache felt as though it had settled down for keeps. Too much worry. But things would work out, sooner or later. They would have to work out. And when the time came, he would explain the whole preposterous situation to Dick Stowell.

He yawned, blinked tired eyes, blinked again. He pressed the electric switch and in the sudden darkness groped his way to the window. He had been right. There was a flashlight bobbing up and down on the grounds. The light crawled like a groping finger toward the window of Noah's bedroom. Halted there.

Then, in the quiet of the night, there was the faint sound of a bell. Noah must be summoning Max. Without stopping for an overcoat, Peter ran across his studio and bedroom, down the corridor, clattered down the stairs. Out of doors he stopped for a moment to adjust his eyes to the darkness. The cold cut through his dinner jacket like a knife. He had been a fool not to provide himself with some sort of a weapon. He had not even bothered to pick up a flashlight.

He raced around the house, crashed headlong into a flying figure, and was tossed aside. The other man thudded on. Dazed for a moment, Peter turned to pursue the intruder, and realized that he was outmatched both in strength and in speed.

He ran across the grounds to the guesthouse where all the lights were now blazing. He could hear raised voices.

". . . never have prowlers here," Max was insisting. He was still only half awake and he was trying to conceal his impatience over what he considered the fantasies of a sick man.

Peter called, and Max, only partially dressed, admitted him. Noah was sitting upright in bed.

"What's going on?" Peter asked.

"Mr. Jones rang for me," Max explained. "He thought someone was trying to see into the guesthouse. I was just telling him—"

"Mr. Jones is quite right," Peter said. "I saw the flashlight on the grounds from the studio and I had a head-on collision with the guy."

Max was startled. "Then I'd better take a look around," he said.

"At the rate he was traveling, he'll be halfway to Canada by now."

"Want me to call the police?"

"No," Peter said.

"No," Noah echoed.

For a long moment the two men exchanged a questioning look. When Peter started back to the house he was whistling thoughtfully to himself.

I

It was late next morning when Nancy awakened from a deep and dreamless sleep. For a moment she looked around the unfamiliar room in bewilderment. Then her eyes fell on the platinum wedding ring, and recollections of the previous day came flooding into her mind. She had married Peter Gerard. For the next few weeks, perhaps months, she must pretend to be a happy wife and she must learn to be a competent and gracious mistress of his home.

At the thought she quailed. The task ahead seemed insurmountable. Then she remembered Noah, who might have a chance to regain his health and his memory in these new surroundings. He might even find an absorbing interest.

"Good morning, Mrs. Gerard," she said cheerfully to herself. "It's up to you, my girl. You pull yourself together. You can make this a dismal swamp if you are sorry for yourself, or you can make it a gay adventure. Remember that wise teacher who said, 'What happens to you doesn't matter; it's what you do about what happens.' "

When she put her finger on the bell beside her bed she was smiling confidently. Then, in sudden recollection, she got up, and ran to unlock her door. A locked door on her wedding night! Every servant would know within an hour. The whole village would hear rumors within days. Little things like that could ruin the whole structure Peter was trying to build. From now on she would have to be more careful. And she would not bother to lock her door again. Whatever Peter's plans might be, she was not included in them.

And a very good thing, too, she told herself firmly. Nonetheless, she paused for a moment to inspect herself in the long triple mirror of her dressing table, black hair tumbling down to her waist, black eyes sparkling, lips scarlet with health, cheeks flushed with sleep.

"I look all right," she told herself, with a confidence that had sprung into being the night before from the expression in the eyes of two young men. "Zombie, indeed!"

She pulled on a plain blue flannel robe over her nightgown; not much like a trousseau, she admitted, but it was all she had.

Helen came in with a heavily laden breakfast tray, set it on the table, removed silver covers and began to pour coffee. With an awkward gesture she upset scalding coffee on Nancy's robe.

She ran for a towel, mopped up the coffee with shaking hands, saying over and over, "I'm so sorry. I'm so sorry."

"Don't bother about it," Nancy said. "It's old and worn out. We were married in such a hurry that I didn't have time to get a trousseau." She looked at the girl who hovered uncertainly beside the table, a slim girl with too sensitive a face, her eyes hidden by the ugly, thick-lensed glasses.

"What is it, Helen?" she asked quietly. "You've never been a maid before. I don't think you've ever worked before. You are frightened." There was a long silence. Nancy tried again. "Can you tell me what it is? It's true that you are frightened, isn't it?"

"No, not really, madam."

"Can I help you? I'm not an ogre, you know."

Helen hesitated. Something in Nancy's warmly sympathetic expression made her explain. Her mother had died some years ago. Her father had never remarried. He was a hardworking physician, "Just a country doctor," he said bitterly of himself. He had wanted to specialize in nervous disorders but, because of his wife's extravagance, he had had to spend all his time plodding along. And now it was probably too late.

As Nancy heard the story unfold, she watched Helen's hands gripping each other tightly, but she did not look into her face. Helen was like a shy bird that would take wing at the slightest alarming movement.

"I suppose, really," Helen said slowly, encouraged by Nancy's attention, "my father became embittered. He got to the point where he felt all women were grasping and selfish. We've never had any social life and I am too shy to make friends on my own.

"I know I've been a burden to him but I didn't have any money to go away. Or any training. But yesterday, after my father told me I was a—a blasted nuisance—I packed a suitcase and left home and just started along the avenue, asking for work at every house.

"You see," she added naïvely, "we don't know the people on the avenue and they don't know us. The wealthy ones go to the big doctors in the city."

"But you'll have to tell him where you are," Nancy pointed out. "It's not fair to worry your father. He is probably out of his mind with anxiety about you."

"More probably," Helen said, "he wouldn't notice I had gone if it weren't for the fact that he'll have to prepare his own meals. But he would make me go back. And I hate it. I hate it! He doesn't really want me, you know."

"Don't worry about that. You aren't going back," Nancy said crisply. "I have an idea."

"But he would be so humiliated at my becoming a maid that my position would be impossible. So," she added in all fairness, "would his."

He doesn't seem to mind humiliating you, Nancy thought, but she said, "We'll call you my secretary. He shouldn't mind that. Anyhow, I'm not used to having a maid. And I'll work things out with your father. I was planning to get in touch with a local physician, anyhow, in case my brother should need someone."

"Oh, madam!"

Nancy smiled at her. "From now on, Mrs. Gerard will do. And get out of that dowdy dress, for heaven's sake! Now sit down, Helen, and we'll make some plans. And lists."

Helen pulled up a second chair and seated herself shyly, pushing up the heavy glasses as though they hurt her. She was still half frightened, but there was a trembling hope about her that made Nancy want to shake the girl's father in a rage. He thought women were selfish, did he? What did he think he was, ignoring his daughter, neglecting her, cutting her off from affection and the chance of any personal life of her own?

"Are you sure you need a secretary?" Helen asked timidly.

Nancy leaned back in her chair, laughing. "You," she declared, "are going to be the answer to a prayer. You are going to be a companion."

Seeing Helen's perplexed look, Nancy laughed again. A bride on her honeymoon needing a hired companion! No wonder Helen was baffled.

"Not my companion," she said. "My brother's."

"But suppose he doesn't want a companion. Suppose he doesn't like the idea."

"He'll loathe it," Nancy told her exuberantly. "He will fight it—and you—tooth and nail."

"But—"

"You leave it to me." Nancy was confident.

Helen made a final effort. "I'm not a nurse, you know."

"I should hope not. It's not a nurse Noah needs; it's a challenge."

II

Nancy and Peter met for the first time that day at luncheon. In the presence of the impassive butler and waitress the meeting might have been awkward. Fortunately, there was a great deal to talk about. Snow had fallen heavily during the night. There were already fourteen inches and no indication of a letup. Peter had been helping Max dig a path from the main house to the guesthouse. He was getting out of condition, he said, and he needed the exercise. So far, Nancy had not been able to see Noah, though she had spoken to him on the telephone.

"He sounded fine," she told Peter.

"He is fine," he assured her. "I saw him myself just a few minutes ago. Sorry I had to take Max away from him but he'll be busy most of the afternoon with the snowplow, clearing the driveway and sanding it."

Peter's face darkened as he spoke. *Watching the snowplow go by for my daily excitement,* Cynthia had said.

"After lunch," Nancy told him, "I'd like to discuss something with you."

He raised his brows in a mute question. "Whenever you like," he said, "I'm sorry you have to be snowbound on your first day in Simonton. I'm afraid it will give you a poor impression of the village as a dull place."

"Dull!" she exclaimed incredulously. "It's so beautiful I can't keep away from the windows. Those hemlocks with their arms piled high with snow. It's breathtaking."

"Then you don't mind the rigors of winter in a New England village," he said in an odd voice.

"You forget how long I lived in Switzerland. About all I brought back with me were skiing outfits. I can't wait to get out."

A faint tinkle of silver at the sideboard reminded Peter of the listening ears. He laughed. "Darling, I'm afraid you are going to find me an awful duffer on skis compared with you."

"We aren't competing. And imagine if I were to try to rival you at painting. When are you going to show me your work, darling?"

"Whenever you like."

All in all, he thought, as he took her through his rather spartan bedroom and into the studio, the meal had gone very well. Nothing to arouse any question or suspicion in the minds of the servants as to their real relationship. Then, as they walked into the studio, he stopped short. On the easel was the unfinished portrait of Cynthia, which he had brought up from New York weeks before. Without a word he removed it, stacked it with others on the floor, facing the wall.

"Now show me," Nancy said eagerly, as though she had not been aware of the face of the smiling blond girl and recognized it. How he had idealized her! Until that day at the Museum he could never have seen her as she was. Even in those fleeting seconds when she had looked at the canvas, she had seen the gentleness, the sweetness, a kind of helplessness that had been conspicuously absent when she had overheard Cynthia speak.

"You really want to see them?" Peter was taken aback. "We aren't on public display now. You can relax."

"But I want to see them. Though if there's anything finer than that landscape—as though you had snatched a single moment of time and caught it forever."

"But that's what I always aim at," he said in a tone of surprise. "Whatever you see is a happening, unique. Something that will never occur again in exactly the same way."

"Not just a happening, though," Nancy said slowly, as he set a canvas on the easel. There was a small house on a desolate prairie. The ground was nearly dark from a storm gathering in the sky. A last gleam of sunlight touched the house. In another moment the storm would strike, the house would be demolished. "It's the meaning of the happening you look for, isn't it?"

"I suppose so." He removed the canvas, put up another. This time he had caught Max absorbed in a book, looking up with abstracted eyes as though pursuing a thought.

One by one, Peter displayed his paintings.

"That's the lot," he said at last. "You've been very patient."

"Patient," she said so impatiently that he laughed. "You must know how good you are. And you've already found your own medium, your own viewpoint, your own technique. I think I'd recognize your brushwork anywhere. Oh, Peter, what genius you have."

"Hey! That's a big word. Let's not abuse it." Before she could protest, he stood back for her to pass him. "You had something to discuss with me?" The moment that had given them a shared interest was gone; she was now a stranger in his private domain.

In her sitting room, he said, "Well?"

It wasn't an encouraging sound but Nancy spoke eagerly. "Two things, really. When I talked to Noah on the phone he told me he had had a prowler last night."

Peter nodded. "I think someone was trying to find out whether your brother really exists, whether the whole explanation for our being here is a fabrication. I don't believe there will be any further trouble. I've taken care of that."

Taken care of what, Nancy wondered, but she did not speak the words aloud. For a little while in his studio Peter had been a reachable man. Now he was remote again. He might as well wear a sign reading, "No trespassing," she thought resentfully.

"I hate doing this to Noah," Peter said. "I practically promised him sanctuary up here. But it may be necessary, sooner or later, for him to make an appearance."

"Oh, Peter, that would be cruel!"

"There's more at stake, Nancy, than the susceptibilities of Noah Jones. A great deal more. If I can spare him the ordeal, I will. Otherwise—"

"Otherwise, you'll make use of him." She did not try to conceal her bitterness, her antagonism.

"Just as you and I are making use of each other," he reminded her blandly. "You said you had two things on your mind." Leaning back against the mantel he looked down at the smoldering face. The banked fires were certainly kindling into flame. It occurred to him that this unpredictable wife of his might cause some unforeseen problems.

"Oh," she said, "it's about Helen, the maid Mrs. Henning employed yesterday to look after me and my nonexistent wardrobe."

"Something must be done about that at once."

"Don't worry, something has been done. Helen and I made out a fairly comprehensive order and telephoned it to New York this morning, with instructions that it was to be delivered at once."

"Well, what about the girl?" He sounded impatient. "If she isn't satisfactory, there's no need to keep her, you know."

Nancy, breathing fire over Dr. Ferrell's ill treatment, told him Helen's story.

"Get that girl back home where she belongs, and do it at once," he said decisively. "The last thing I want at this point is any trouble in the village. And by keeping the girl here against her father's will—"

"I have an idea about that," Nancy told him.

"Every time you get an idea," he said gravely, but with laughter in his eyes, "I get cold shivers down my spine."

"You're just quoting Noah," Nancy told him. "Anyhow, Helen's father is a physician. I'm going to call him about Noah. Then I'll say that Helen is staying here as a—a secretary. He won't mind that."

"And what do you want with a secretary?"

"I'll think of something."

"That's just what I am afraid of."

Unexpectedly, they both began to laugh. Peter broke off as he saw Murch hovering in the doorway.

"Mr. Hacker is here," the butler said. "He would like to interview madam."

Peter hesitated for a moment. "All right, we might as well get it over. Come along, Mrs. Gerard. This is going to be a joint interview."

He took Nancy's hand, pulled her to her feet, and led her down the corridor. They were still hand in hand as they went down the stairs.

"Think first and speak afterwards," he told her, his voice just above a whisper.

EIGHT

JOE HACKER was waiting in the library. He was a slim, alert-looking man of forty, with wiry energy, a sardonic expression around his mouth, and a dreamer's eyes. Nancy corrected her first impression: the eyes of a dreamer— or a fanatic.

"Hello, Hacker," Peter said. "Nancy, this is Joe Hacker. My wife."

Hacker's lips puckered in a whistle. "And me without a camera! Mr. Gerard, you have my most enthusiastic congratulations, and you'll have the envy of every man who sees your wife."

Nancy laughed as she shook hands with him.

"And I've never even heard of you before," Hacker complained. "Mr. Gerard certainly kept you under wraps so no one else would have a chance."

"But I've heard of you, Mr. Hacker," she assured him. "Dick Stowell was here last night." She was aware of Peter's sudden tension, as though he were trying to convey a warning. "He gave you a tremendous build-up. A Pulitzer Prize winner. Tell me, what did you do to earn that?"

"Just a series of articles on housing. Very dull stuff actually. What I'd like to know—"

"But I should think," she said, "with a record like that, all the metropolitan papers would have wanted you."

"Oh, I could have stayed in the city, of course. The

71

thing is that I've always wanted to run a country paper. I'm just a small-town boy at heart. How long have you—"

"But isn't newspaper work less exciting, less stimulating here than in New York?" Nancy leaned forward in her chair, the great dark eyes fixed on Hacker's face. Peter's tension had relaxed. He was listening in growing amusement.

"It's people who provide the real interest," Hacker explained. "In New York they are just names. A big headline today and gone tomorrow. In a way, most stories remain unfinished. You don't know how it all came out. But in a little place like this they are all human beings. The problems are direct and personal, not cut down to a news item; they are life being lived before your eyes. You get to the bottom of the situation. At least," he hesitated, "sometimes you do. Even a village like Simonton has its—undercurrents."

Peter looked at him quickly, started to speak, changed his mind. After a moment he asked casually, "Who's around now? I don't want my wife to feel isolated. Of course, I know Dick Stowell's in town."

The editor nodded. "Stowell is one of the best. And he works like a dog, though he makes light of his own achievements. Night after night, I've seen the lights burning in his cottage and heard his typewriter clattering away."

"Who else is here?"

"Not as many people as usual, and few you'd be likely to know well. With all those forecasts of a severe winter—and for once the weather experts seem to have hit it on the nose—there's been an exodus. The village is practically at a standstill. Oh, the Wheelers are still here, of course. They rarely go away for more than a few weeks. I suppose they think Simonton would collapse without them."

"The Wheelers," Peter explained to Nancy, "are an elderly couple. Their house is almost directly across the avenue from us. The house has been standing since Colonial times. Once a year it is open to the public."

"The Wheelers," Hacker commented, "still live in the Colonial era. In their quiet way, they resist anything in the way of progress."

"I suppose that happens to people as they grow old if they haven't kept interested in their world," Nancy said.

"It hasn't happened to the Mortons," the editor told her. "They go to the opposite extreme. Anything as old as day before yesterday they want no part of. Progress is Morton's keynote."

Peter smiled at Nancy. "This up-and-coming gent whom Hacker is describing is a retired industrialist. Heavy machinery, I think. I suspect he would have preferred retiring to Miami Beach but his wife balked. She said she had had enough official entertaining to last for the rest of her life. She wanted to live in a small town—she was born in one, somewhere in the Midwest—and have some neighbors who were really friends, not just business associates, and plant a garden."

"That strikes me as rather a nice program," Nancy said. "I suppose it's never too late to put down roots."

"If that's the way you feel about it," Hacker declared, "your husband is even luckier than I thought he was. And that's saying something." There was a note of unhappiness in his voice that made Peter study him thoughtfully. "Right now, Mrs. Morton is acting as lady patroness to our local artist."

"Who is that?" Peter asked.

"A fellow named Miller. Philip Miller. He keeps his chin above water by doing commercial art but he's trying to do some serious work as well."

"I don't remember anyone like that," Peter said.

"He's new since your time, I think. Well, Mrs. Gerard —"

"How on earth do you find news to fill a paper during the winter months when the village seems to have gone to sleep?" she asked eagerly.

In answer to her deft questions, Hacker went on talking about the fascination of small-town news editing. The chimes of a little gold clock on the mantel startled him.

"Good Lord! I have a paper to get out." He stood up. "But next time," and he smiled at Nancy, "you are going to be interviewed. Not me."

Peter laughed outright.

As Nancy held out her hand Hacker said, "I hope you'll like Simonton as much as I do."

"How can I help it!" she exclaimed. "It's so beautiful."

"I wish," the editor said, a wistful note in his voice, "you could sell my wife on it. Nothing for her to do, you know, but sit around the inn all day. And when there's a storm like this one——"

"I'll call on her," Nancy said.

"That would be swell, Mrs. Gerard, and I can tell you right now that anything a Gerard says carries a lot of weight around here." Something odd in his voice made Nancy look at him. He did not notice the look; he was watching Peter as though, Nancy thought in surprise, he did not like him at all.

"Well, I have an idea," she began.

"Look out, Hacker," Peter warned him. "When this girl has an idea, someone is in for trouble." He accompanied Hacker to the door where they talked for a few moments about the storm and the driving problems involved.

Nancy picked up the telephone and asked for Dr. Ferrell's number.

"Dr. Ferrell's office? . . . This is Mrs. Peter Gerard . . . That's right. *Mrs.* Gerard. My husband and I have brought my brother up here to recuperate from a serious illness. I would be so grateful if the doctor could come by to see him as soon as possible . . . No, not an emergency. Just that it might be useful for him to have an understanding of the case if any complication should arise . . . Four o'clock? That will be fine . . . Oh, and will you please inform Dr. Ferrell that his daughter is staying with us for a while?"

In the doorway, Peter stood looking at her. "You really handled Hacker." He chuckled. "I'll bet it's the first time the editor ever had the tables turned on him and got interviewed."

Nancy laughed up at him. "It was the only way I could think of to stop him from asking questions I didn't know how to answer. And I had an idea——"

"Oh, no!"

"You couldn't have done any better," she flamed.
"How right you are."

I

It was true, Peter admitted to himself, that he couldn't have handled the interview with Hacker better than Nancy. He couldn't have done so well. Her eager and obviously genuine interest had elicited a lot of information. In fact, Nancy was proving herself to be a valuable colleague rather than the necessary stage prop he had anticipated.

One thing had been made apparent during the talk with Hacker. The interview, and Peter grinned to himself, in which the editor was the interviewed, did bring out that practically all the leading citizens of Simonton were away for the winter. That should simplify the task for him.

He set up a fresh canvas on his easel and, while he mixed paints on his palette, he recalled what he had been told about the conspiracy whose focal point was Simonton, Connecticut. *Find those men for us,* were his instructions, *and find them in a hurry.*

Somewhere in Simonton subversive propaganda was being written and printed. Somewhere in the village was the core of a conspiracy to intensify discontent and to rally the malcontents: the embittered, the failures, the neurotics; they were to join under a single banner, the nucleus of a strong drive for political power in which those who regarded themselves as the spokesmen and leaders would actually be the puppets. The pattern was familiar. It flourished, at a risk to all civilization, at least five times within the present century, both in Europe and the Far East.

Although the directives were being mailed in New York, an investigator traced their source to Simonton, and then the whole thing came to a standstill.

How had it been traced to Simonton? Why did it come to a standstill? These were questions to which Peter had demanded an answer. He was not going into the thing blindfolded.

It was Foster, the FBI man, who provided the explanation. One of their operatives, he said, had been on the job;

he had in his possession all the information he had collected; he telephoned in jubilation to say he was coming in with it.

"Well?" Peter demanded impatiently.

"He didn't show up." Foster's voice was flat and expressionless. "Next day he was found in a Bowery flophouse. No papers on him. Nothing. No, he hadn't been murdered. Apparently he had collapsed from a heart attack as a result of shock, and he'd been moved to the Bowery, left there in the hope that he would be taken for some poor fellow on Skid Row. So—we had to start over. All we knew was the fact that Simonton was the headquarters from which the stuff was coming."

Peter went over the facts of the conspiracy, as they had been uncovered. Student groups in universities, popular lecturers, a few newspaper editors, commentators for radio and television, political groups, all claiming strong democratic tendencies—

"Like Hitler," Peter interrupted.

"Like Hitler," the Personage agreed grimly.

What had become increasingly evident was that, though none of the groups seemed to be related in any way, they were all following the same general lines, or, more correctly, they were being told what to say. The American people had no friends in the world. The principles on which the nation had been based were false. What was needed was to end the complicated and inefficient democratic machinery. Almost unnoticed, except in isolated instances, the ferment had begun to work, the number of malcontents was growing.

As he thought of it, Peter put aside his palette impatiently and began to pace back and forth, trying to control his anger. Never, at any time, in any part of the world, had people lived as well and hopefully, as free to express their minds and to develop as individuals, as in the United States. Of course, there were weak spots, but at least we didn't cover them up, we didn't pretend they weren't there. We didn't hide our problems behind the Iron Curtain, we didn't shut our citizens behind a wall, we didn't put dissenters in concentration camps. We admitted our mistakes and shortcomings publicly and tried to do better.

What more, Peter wondered savagely, did people expect? If they wanted things improved, why didn't they do something about it? Why look for a scapegoat? It was their country. Let them go to work to make it better.

He controlled his pointless rage with an effort. That was a waste of energy. This ugly thing had to be stopped and he had been elected to track down the people who were attempting to undermine their country, like mice nibbling at the foundation. No, not mice. Rats.

So far he had no clue to the identity of the people he was seeking. Obviously there was intelligence at work and a sound financial backing. The trouble was that, though he had no clue to the identity of these people, they had a clue to him. He wondered how much they had learned at the Fourteenth Street office. Someone must know of his visit there. That could be the only explanation for last night's intruder. Someone was interested enough in checking Peter's reason for being in Simonton, for postponing a diplomatic career, to try to investigate the guesthouse during a heavy storm, checking on Noah's presence there.

But that, Peter realized suddenly, could not have been learned by staking out the Fourteenth Street place. At the time of his visit there, Peter himself had not known of Noah's existence. That meant the telephone must have been tapped. No doubt, that was why he had been given a special emergency number, which was known to only three people.

Take care of yourself, Brooks had said cheerfully. He had done his best, Peter thought, but he did not forget that the man who had traced the conspiracy to Simonton had died. He pushed the thought aside. This was his job and he had to handle it the best he could.

There were few of the villagers who were not old-time residents, people whose parents and grandparents had settled there. The more ambitious young ones moved away to the cities. There were few whose names and faces and backgrounds he did not know. It seemed reasonably safe to assume that no wide-scale conspiracy could be carried on among them. In the first place, everyone knew everyone else's business, knew their habits, knew their income. Any change would be instantly noticed.

This left only a handful of possible suspects. Peter went over them in his mind:

a) The Mortons.

b) The unknown painter—Miller, wasn't it?

c) After a moment's hesitation, Peter added the name of Joe Hacker. For all his assumed enthusiasm for small-town editing, he didn't seem to be happy about it. And it was an odd spot for a man of his brilliant professional standing.

Three names. Peter racked his brains but he could think of no one else who seemed even remotely possible.

Now what was the first step? Peter recalled that he had a bride. He would hold open house to introduce her to her neighbors. Perhaps when he saw these people together he would get some ideas.

Nancy was not in her sitting room and Peter found her in his mother's morning room on the first floor, talking to the housekeeper. He glanced at the drab, badly dressed girl in the corner, wearing ugly yellow glasses. That must be the problem child, Helen Ferrell.

"Are you busy?" he asked.

Mrs. Henning got to her feet. "Just through, sir. I've been discussing menus with madam."

Murch appeared. "Dr. Ferrell," he announced.

Helen gasped. Nancy smiled encouragingly at her. "You run along. I'll talk to your father." She turned to Murch. "Will you show the doctor in?"

Helen scurried out and when Murch had gone, Peter said, scowling, "I told you to get rid of that girl."

"It will be all right, Peter. Honestly it will."

"I can't afford to stir up the slightest dislike or resentment here, Nancy."

"You already have."

"What does that mean?" He came farther into the room.

"Joe Hacker. I saw the way he looked at you. He doesn't like you at all."

"We-ell," Peter said slowly. "Oh, by the way, I want to hold open house and have you meet the Simonton people. There won't be many but at least it's a start. We can work out the details with Mrs. Henning." After a moment he asked rather irritably, "What's wrong with that?"

"I was wondering—when we get the annulment—won't it be more awkward if you have been fitting me into your life here?"

"What choice do I have? If this were a real marriage I certainly wouldn't be keeping you under wraps, as Hacker put it."

"I suppose not."

"Dr. Ferrell," Murch said, and stood aside to let the doctor enter the room.

He was a thickset man in his early fifties with a tight mouth whose corners pulled downward. From the worn bag in his hand to his shoes he was shabby. A disappointed, disillusioned, embittered man, Peter thought. Embittered. It was from such people, those with a real or fancied grievance, that the malcontents were recruited.

Dr. Ferrell was somewhat intimidated by the surroundings in which he found himself. As a result he held himself stiffly, on the defensive.

Nancy came forward to meet him, hand outstretched. "Dr. Ferrell, I am Anne Gerard. How nice of you to come so promptly. This is my husband."

Whatever the country doctor had expected it had not been Nancy's loveliness with its essential simplicity and warmth. Peter was amused to see him unbend slightly. When he had shaken hands with the doctor, Peter withdrew. He was beginning to realize that Nancy was fully able to cope with the situation without his assistance.

II

Actually, it was Dr. Ferrell who needed assistance. At Nancy's suggestion he pulled up a chair, his bag at his feet.

"Before I see your brother, Mrs. Gerard, I'd like to know what Helen is doing here, and how long you expect her to stay."

The great dark eyes were extremely direct. "She is going to help me with some plans I've been making, and she'll stay, of course, as long as she cares to."

"It didn't occur to her that I might need someone

myself," he said bitterly. "I know all women are selfish but—"

"But," the black eyes blazed now, there were red spots of color in Nancy's cheeks, "you called her a blasted nuisance. You've made a slave of her, a meek little slave without any self-confidence, any life of her own, any affection from her own father."

Before he could speak she stormed on. "Selfishness, Dr. Ferrell, is not a quality confined to women. Perhaps I— we—will be able to give Helen some confidence, make her an independent person, help her to be less shy and unhappy and frightened."

"Frightened!" he expostulated. "What has she to be afraid of?"

"Being unwanted. And loneliness. I know a lot about loneliness myself, Doctor."

The tired, disillusioned eyes studied her. "Why does this concern you?"

"Because I think it's part of a woman's job to help a little. There is so much unhappiness. And sometimes the remedy is easy if anyone cares enough."

Even when he smiled, the steeply downward curve of the lips did not alter. They simply deepened at the corners. "You," he said, with a glance around the beautiful room, "are one of the lucky ones."

"I've always believed we make our own luck, Dr. Ferrell."

"Do you, indeed?"

"At least, I'd like to think so. Well," she stood up. "I'll get my coat and some boots. My brother is in the guesthouse."

By the time Murch had helped the doctor into the shabby overcoat, Nancy ran lightly down the stairs, wearing her black wool coat, boots on her feet, a scarf tied over her head. He picked up his bag to follow her.

She halted suddenly. "Before you see my brother I should explain that his face is horribly scarred by an automobile accident in which his wife was killed. He is morbidly sensitive about it. If you require any of his medical history you can get it from Dr. Ross Warburton."

Ferrell was impressed. "He has a great reputation."

"It was his idea, really, that we come up here, get Noah out of the hopsital, shake him out of his apathy."

"I don't move in your circles," the doctor said bitterly, "but I understood that Mr. Gerard had been offered a big diplomatic post in Europe."

"And I hope he'll be able to accept one soon. But Peter agrees with me that human needs come first."

The wind was stronger now, blowing snow like small pieces of ice against their faces. They bent under its force, fighting their way along the path to the guesthouse.

Nancy knocked at the door and called. As Noah answered, "Come in," in his big, resonant voice, she opened the door.

The cottage was tiny, with one room and bath on each floor, and a small kitchenette off the downstairs room. The couch bed on which Noah slept had been made up with a tailored cover of dark red to match a big leather armchair. A cheerful fire crackled in the grate. Noah, wearing a black and silver silk dressing gown that seemed oddly theatrical in this simple setting, was sunk in the deep chair before the fire, brooding, an unopened book on his lap.

He looked around and when he saw a stranger behind Nancy he stiffened, his hands tightened on the carved arms of his chair.

Nancy stamped snow off her boots and came forward to kiss him, apparently unaware of his tension.

"This," she said cheerfully, "is Dr. Ferrell. My brother, Noah Jones. I thought it would be a good idea for you two to get acquainted in case you should need him at any time."

"I don't," Noah said ill-temperedly, "need any more doctors."

Ferrell set down his bag and pulled up a chair facing Noah. The man who had been so uncertain in a social position was in command of the situation here.

"You certainly don't look as though you did," he said easily.

"The way I look—" Noah began.

Ferrell leaned closer, studied Noah's face, while Nancy bit her lips. Suppose she had made a mistake!

"You must have had Windrom do that plastic surgery," the doctor said with professional enthusiasm. "Marvelous job. There's not a man in the country who equals him. I'd say those scars will disappear almost without trace. I suppose he plans a final operation on the jaw."

His manner was as casual as though Noah had cut himself shaving. Slowly Noah's hands relaxed their tight grip on the chair arms.

"Yes, it was Windrom. The final operation will be performed whenever I'm physically fit for it. Or if ever."

"Well, that's up to you, of course." Ferrell was matter-of-fact. "After I've talked to Warburton I'll give you a checkup. But I'd say there's nothing wrong now that you can't handle yourself. Get out of that chair and begin to take some exercise. Not too much at a time, of course. I'll show you what to do. As soon as you've picked up some strength you'll get on your feet and start walking again. Preferably out of doors."

"In this weather?" Noah asked, struggling against change.

"Hell, yes," the doctor said unsympathetically. "You are a good healthy specimen. Too thin. Too nervous. When you begin to exercise you'll get stronger. When you get out in the fresh air you'll build up an appetite and put on weight."

"I can't get out," Noah said flatly. "I don't like to see people or have them see me."

The doctor shrugged. "Well, unfortunately, there's no prescription I know that can supply a man with guts."

Nancy gave an angry exclamation and then saw the expression on her brother's face. She fell silent.

"You don't go in for the bedside manner, do you?" Noah sounded surprised but amused.

"I never thought it helped anyone to be smothered in kindness," Ferrell retorted. He looked at Nancy and a reluctant, half-guilty smile deepened the corners of his tight mouth.

Nancy found herself smiling back. Whatever Ferrell's shortcomings as a father, he knew his job as a doctor. She fastened the collar of her coat, feeling lighthearted once more.

"You don't need me any longer. If you want anything just call the house."

NINE

THAT EVENING there were no unexpected visitors. Coffee was served in the morning room at the back of the house. After Nancy had described the doctor's visit, Peter talked about his plans for the open house.

"There are comparatively few people here," he said, "so it will be a simple affair, perhaps twenty people or so. I especially want the Wheelers, the Mortons, Dick Stowell, the Hackers." He thought for a moment. "We'll try to get Mrs. Morton's tame artist to come if we can manage without making too much of a point of it."

"And Dr. Ferrell?" Nancy suggested.

"He's just the regular practitioner for the village. He has never really fitted on the avenue."

"How do you know? Has anyone asked him?"

Peter's brow rose in surprise. "I thought you were breathing fire about the man."

"I don't like the way he has behaved toward his daughter but I have a feeling he's a good doctor; at least, he's going to be good for Noah. And for heaven's sake, Peter, can't we tear down the barrier between the avenue and the rest of the village?"

"It appears," he said in amusement, "that we not only can; we're going to."

"Well, I—"

"Have an idea." They both spoke at once and suddenly they were laughing.

It had been Peter's intention, as soon as the servants were out of the way, to go up to his studio. Instead, he dropped another log on the fire, lighted a pipe, and rested his head on the back of his chair. There was something curiously peaceful about Nancy's quiet presence. For a beautiful woman she made no attempt to exploit her looks and their inevitable effect on men.

At length she broke the silence. "I wonder what it is," she said in her lovely low voice, "about an open fire that is so comforting on a winter night, even when a house is warm without it."

"Some race memory, perhaps, of our days in caves, when fire was a protection from wild animals as well as from the cold." He turned his head lazily, the pipe loosely held in one articulate hand. The firelight emphasized the planes of his face, the deep-set eyes, the bold lines of eyebrows. "I couldn't count the times I've sat before this fire, listening to my mother tell stories. And my father sat here before that, and his father, and his father. Though it's unlikely the house was anywhere near as comfortable in those days. It took a lot of guts for those pioneers to carve a civilization out of New England with its harsh climate."

"Do we still have them, Peter?"

"Have what?" He turned to look at her. She was staring at the fire and he watched her profile. There was a strength about her that he had never found in Cynthia. It had, to some extent, been Cynthia's apparent helplessness that had appealed to him, made him feel so protective. What he had found, in the long run, was hardness. But Nancy's strength, a kind of gay courage, was gentle; there was no hardness in her.

"Pioneers," she said. "I suppose I really mean the spirit of pioneers. Or are we too civilized to need it any more?"

"We'll never be that civilized, and we'll always need it. If it isn't forests and mountains and rivers and savages we have to conquer, it's poverty and hatred and misunderstanding and ignorance. There's always a new jungle to clear. There always will be."

"Doesn't that discourage you?"

Peter laughed. "I like a good fight. I come from fighting stock."

"Tell me about your people, Peter."

Somewhat to his own surprise, Peter found himself talking about his family, about the long bitter struggle for survival in the New World; about the difficult building, stone by stone, of a nation that was unlike any other on earth.

"How different our lives have been," she said softly when he had finished. "Always, even when your people were uprooted, they were rooted. No, don't laugh. I mean they carried with them a—a kind of continuity. I don't know how to express it."

"You're doing all right."

"You see, I've always been rootless. Good schools and a pleasant life but—always moving on. You remember poor Jo in that Dickens novel, *Bleak House*? Always moving on. So many countries, so many ways of life. I don't mean they weren't good or that they didn't teach me a lot, but, instead of having roots, I'm more like an air plant."

"Some air plants are very beautiful," Peter said. He added abruptly, "Good night, Nancy." A few minutes later she heard him going upstairs.

I

Next day the sky cleared and the sun came out, blazing on the snow-covered trees and bushes, and the long irregular lines of stone walls that curved like monstrous snakes across the white fields.

At lunchtime Nancy, again wearing the plain blue dress, discussed her plans with Peter.

"This afternoon," she said, "I'm going to call on Mrs. Hacker at the inn. It's too lovely to stay indoors."

"I'll have Max drive you."

"How far is it?"

"Less than half a mile."

"Then I'll walk."

"Max has nothing to do."

"He's helping Noah with some exercises, trying to get him on his feet. Anyhow, I'd rather walk. You can see so much more that way and I haven't really seen Simonton at all."

Once out of doors, Nancy walked briskly because of the cold, her eyes absorbing the stately beauty of the old Connecticut houses along the avenue. Most of them seemed to be unoccupied except for caretakers. They were all set so far back on their grounds and so carefully screened by shrubbery that they had a privacy and seclusion that is becoming increasingly difficult to achieve, particularly so close to a great city.

One house was very different from all the rest, a small dark cottage with a high chimney and small leaded windows. It must, Nancy thought, date back to the 1600's, one of the earliest houses in the state. Unlike the others, this one was set almost on the sidewalk. It belonged to a day when easy access to a road had been imperative in winter.

At length, she came to a crossroads. This, she remembered, was where Max had turned on the day of their arrival. A tall stone clock tower marked the time as it had done for generations. Across the street Nancy found herself in the village proper. On the north side of the street were the inn and a few large but run-down houses. On the south side there was a small but lovely brick church and beyond it there were several shops. All of them had been designed in an early Colonial style to retain the charm of the village. Nancy walked along the south side, noticing the small market, a drugstore, a bookshop, and a bow window, like an illustration for *Cranford,* displaying a spinet and a lute.

As she walked around the dead-end street she saw a small cottage that faced the street but which, at the back, had a magnificent view of the hills. In spite of the cold she stood enjoying the view. Then the cottage door opened and Dick Stowell came out, pulling on a thick sweater. In that low doorway he looked bigger than ever.

"Hello," he called cheerfully. "I thought it must be you. Come in and see how the other half lives. You'll rest these tired old eyes."

She laughed. "Sorry, I'm on my way to the inn to call on Mrs. Hacker. I promised her husband."

"Lady Bountiful," Dick said lightly. Then he saw her expression. "Sorry, I was just joking. How's your brother?"

"Dr. Ferrell says he is doing very well. Just a question of time now and building up his strength. Before we know it, he'll have Noah out shoveling snow."

"Well!" Dick sounded surprised. He added slowly, "Too bad you didn't get a country doctor before. Maybe Peter could have taken that job after all."

Unexpectedly Nancy found her eyes blurred by tears. She wiped them away impatiently. No, of course, she wasn't crying. The wind made her eyes water. She went quickly toward the inn, knowing that Dick was staring after her in perplexity and concern. It isn't my fault, she wanted to tell him; it isn't Noah's fault. I don't blame you for resenting this setback to Peter's career, but it isn't my fault. It isn't. He would be here whether or not he had married me.

The inn was rather self-consciously quaint and charming. On one side of the hallway there was a dining room, on the other a sitting room, with settles beside the fireplace, within which hung a big iron crane. There were old-fashioned rockers, a piecrust table, a spinning wheel in one corner, rag rugs scattered over polished wide floor boards. A jumble of styles and periods, but the effect was delightful.

The room was empty except for a woman who sat knitting before the fire, needles flashing in and out of crimson wool that spilled on her lap. As Nancy closed the front door behind her a man came through the swinging door at the back of the hall. He looked at Nancy, looked in vain for luggage.

"Do you have a reservation?"

"I don't want a room," Nancy said.

He smiled to cover his disappointment. "Not many people come this time of year but it does no harm to hope."

"I came to call on one of your guests, a Mrs. Hacker."

He nodded toward the woman who sat alone in the

sitting room and then the swinging door closed behind him.

At the sound of her name the woman looked up, a plump woman in her middle thirties, with a pleasant face, wearing a brown knit suit that fitted beautifully.

"I am Mrs. Hacker. Are you looking for me?"

Nancy came into the room. "I am Anne Gerard."

Mrs. Hacker got up and held out her hand. "How very nice of you to come! Joe said you spoke of it but, knowing you were just married and all, I didn't really expect that you'd do it." With a hospitable gesture she pulled up a rocking chair.

Nancy dropped her coat on one of the settles and looked around in appreciation. "What a charming place!"

Mrs. Hacker's lips compressed. "Oh, yes, of course. Lots of atmosphere." She did not seem to be enthusiastic about atmosphere. "Joe loves it. Not just the inn, of course; the whole village."

"From what I've seen of it," Nancy said, "I don't blame him." Her eyes fell on the crimson wool. "What an intricate pattern! A sweater?"

"A three-piece knit suit, like the one I'm wearing."

"You made that yourself? It's beautiful. But it must have taken ages."

"I'm glad you like it. Anyhow, I have ages. There's nothing to do here. I try not to complain because this is what makes Joe happy, and that's the chief thing, but knitting is all I've found to keep me busy."

"The inn seems comfortable."

"Oh, it's comfortable," Mrs. Hacker agreed, again without enthusiasm, "but the meals—say what you like, Mrs. Gerard, but anyone gets sick to death of eating out. Sometimes it's all I can do to keep from marching into the kitchen and just taking over. I could get better meals with both hands tied behind my back."

Something in her vigorous tone made Nancy laugh aloud. "You're a born homemaker, aren't you?"

"Well, if I do say it, I'm a good cook. You would never see Joe looking so gaunt if I had the feeding of him, I can tell you that. I know how to cater to his appetite. And then I like puttering around a house, don't you, polishing the furniture until it is like satin, arranging closets so that they look like the pretty ones in the ads, moving things around, now and then; though, I must say, that's something a man doesn't like. Once a piece of furniture is placed, he expects it to stay that way forever."

"Then why don't you get a little house of your own?" Nancy suggested.

Mrs. Hacker's eyes brightened. "Don't think I haven't dreamed of it. And wouldn't I love it! And it would be cheaper in the long run than living at the inn. But Joe needs the car for his work and I have no way to getting around to see houses."

"Let's do it together," Nancy suggested eagerly. "Peter is working hard, preparing for a one-man show in the spring before he is sent abroad again, and my brother is so well looked after he doesn't need me. Anyhow, Dr. Ferrell thinks he'd be better off with a little—uh—judicious neglect. He says there's a point beyond which a patient has to be his own doctor. I wish we had discovered Dr. Ferrell sooner. Anyhow, you can see that I have plenty of time on my hands and I'd love exploring Simonton."

"You mean it?" Mrs. Hacker's face was alight, transformed.

"Of course I mean it."

"Now I can understand why Joe came back practically dithering. First time he's ever made me jealous. He said you weren't just beautiful, you were wonderful."

"Whee!" Nancy laughed. "That will take a lot of living up to." She slipped into her coat. "You start making a list of places and we'll go see them. Oh, and Peter is planning an open house so I can meet his neighbors. I do hope you and your husband will come."

II

The next day was one of activity. In the morning the clothes ordered by Nancy were delivered and she and Helen spent hours opening the big boxes, removing tissue paper, exclaiming and admiring. With Helen's help, Nancy tried them on: evening dresses, afternoon dresses, wool street dresses, suits and sports clothes, shoes and negligees.

She studied herself, her eyes anxious, hoping this was the proper trousseau for the wife of Peter Gerard, hoping she had not spent too much money for it.

Helen, on her knees, with pins in her mouth, helped shorten the skirt of an afternoon dress of dark green with a gold belt.

"Like a glove," she said at last, removing the pins. "It fits like a glove. That color's awfully becoming. But then you can wear anything."

"I have never," Nancy said looking at the open wardrobe where dresses hung on padded, scented hangers, hats perched above in gay boxes, shoes below, carefully treed, "never, never, never, had so many clothes in all my life. Which dress shall I wear for the open house? It will be an afternoon affair, three to six."

Together they examined the dresses. "This one," they said at the same time. It was of sheer white wool, so soft and light as to appear weightless. It dramatized Nancy's black hair and eyes.

"You'll need some ornament with it," Helen said, "to relieve those plain lines."

"I have a pearl necklace. It will be just right. Now about you—"

"Mrs. Gerard!" Helen sat back on her heels, looking up in alarm. She was, Nancy thought, like a little brown wren with great yellow goggle eyes. "You don't expect me to come to your party?"

"Would you mind so much?"

"I'd much rather not; I'd feel so out of place, not knowing people, and it's terribly hard for me to make friends. You don't care?"

Nancy laughed mischievously. "That's what I hoped. We are going to need Max to park cars so I want you to stay with Noah."

"Oh," Helen said blankly.

"His bark is worse than his bite," Nancy assured her.

"Oh." This time the monosyllable was gloomy with foreboding.

"Peter has asked your father to the party."

"He has? No one has ever asked him before to a party on the avenue."

"Then it's time they did. So far as I can tell, he's a fine doctor, a dedicated doctor. People ought to appreciate what they've got."

"How on earth did you persuade him to let me stay here?" Helen asked. She scrambled awkwardly to her feet. As she did so, she brushed against the bed, knocking off her glasses.

This time it was Nancy who said, "Oh," on a long note. She added, "Well, well, well. Why do you wear those horrible things?"

Helen giggled nervously as she slipped the heavy glasses on again. "Once I read a novel of Aldous Huxley's—you remember the one about the shy man who put on a thick beard and it disguised him and made him feel bold as a lion? Well, so I got these—"

"They are a disguise, all right," Nancy said in an odd voice. "But if you think for one minute that they have made you bold as a lion, my girl, you've got another think coming. You haven't the courage of a six-weeks' kitten. You haven't the heart of a mouse!"

The two girls found themselves rocking with laughter. Then Nancy looked at her watch. "I'll have to see Mrs. Henning about some last-minute planning."

"And you really want me to stay with your brother while the party's going on?"

"I really do."

"But suppose—"

"It's up to you, Mouse. Sink or swim."

"Oh."

"But if you must sink, at least do it with a great big splash. If there's anything Noah hates, it's a wee, timid, cowering beastie!"

TEN

THAT EVENING, Nancy wore one of the new dinner dresses, which looked like an orange flame. There were voices in the library when she came downstairs and she found Dick Stowell with Peter.

Dick looked at her and whistled. "Wow!" he said enthusiastically.

Nancy looked quickly at Peter but he said nothing at all. There was an odd expression on his face and she was intuitively aware that the two men had been discussing her. No, she decided, Dick had been talking about Noah and his improved health prospects. He had probably been trying to persuade Peter to think less of his brother-in-law and more of his own career.

"Nancy," Dick said, "I am a very pathetic case. Look at me, fallen away to skin and bone." He stood smiling at her, radiating magnificent health and vitality. "All I have at home is a can of baked beans. Now I appeal to you—"

Nancy laughed. "Did you tell Murch we'll have a guest for dinner?" she asked Peter.

"I didn't need to. Whenever he sees Dick he knows the cadger is looking for a handout."

The two men smiled at each other.

Murch appeared in the doorway and Nancy expected the announcement that dinner was served. Instead, he said, "I'm sorry, sir, there was a telephone message for

you but Max was busy and the waitress took it. She forgot
it."

Peter held out his hand.

"She didn't even write it down, sir." Murch was shaken
out of his imperturbability. "A Miss Cynthia Barbee
called. She said she would be arriving tonight at eight."

Nancy found herself gripping her small petit point
evening bag. She dared not look at Peter. When he spoke
she barely recognized his voice, he was so shaken out of
control.

"She can't come here! Where did she call from?"

"Apparently she didn't say, sir."

"Excuse me." Peter went quickly out of the room. He
wanted to telephone in privacy. In a few minutes Murch
appeared again. "Madam—"

Nancy followed him to the morning room. Peter was
bending over, picking up pieces of a broken pipe. There
was a scar on the exquisite inlaid desk where he had
smashed it. When he looked up his face was ravaged.
How he loved her, Nancy thought.

"I can't reach her," he said in a tone of despair. "She
must be on the way. I can't stop her." He looked at Nancy
as though she were a stranger whom he was seeing for the
first time. "What am I going to do, Nancy? What am I
going to do?"

"Why is she coming, Peter?"

"Because I didn't crawl back as soon as she expected,"
he said harshly, "and I'm a very wealthy man."

"At least—when she knows you are married—she
won't stay."

"But she'll wonder; she'll do a hell of a lot of wondering. Don't you see—"

"I see one thing," Nancy blazed. "She has no right to
expect you to go on loving her. Not after the way she
acted."

He dropped his hands with a helpless gesture. "No, you
don't understand the main problem. She'll know the whole
story is a fake. I planned to come here before I ever heard
of Noah, or," this was an afterthought, "you. God knows
how much harm she can do, if she wants to. And our 'Just
Married' bliss won't stand up for a moment with her."

Nancy's eyes flashed. "How do you know?" she challenged him. "We really haven't worked at it yet."

He gave her the smile that transformed his rather stern face and touched her shoulder lightly. "You're a real fighter, aren't you? Old Reliable, that's what you are, Nancy. Old Reliable." As Murch appeared in the doorway, he said, "All right. Announce dinner in five minutes." When the butler had gone he said, "Wait. I'm going to get the diamond necklace from the safe. I want you to wear it tonight."

He went out of the room. A few minutes later he returned, the necklace dangling between his fingers. He fastened it around her neck. The groom's gift to the bride, Nancy thought. He is doing this to punish Cynthia. She wanted—how she wanted—to tear the thing off and throw it in his face.

I

Only later did it occur to Nancy that Dick Stowell had been singularly unaware of the tension during dinner. He rattled happily along, giving them an hilarious travesty of the plot of his new science fiction novel and an irreverent imitation of the Wheelers presiding over a meeting of the Historical Society. Nancy seconded him as well as she could, but Peter only occasionally emerged from his deep absorption in his own thoughts to make a comment.

Long afterwards, Nancy realized that Dick had been conscious of the tension and that he guessed it was owing to the unexpected arrival of Miss Cynthia Barbee. But his social tact and his high spirits carried them through the meal from crabmeat cocktails to a perfect chocolate soufflé.

The doorbell could not be heard in the small dining room but when Murch, after a short absence, returned and with an automatic glance to check on the activities of the erring waitress, coughed slightly, Nancy found her hands tightening on her napkin, and Peter drew a long breath, bracing himself.

"Miss Barbee."

"Show her into the drawing room, Murch," Nancy said quietly. "We'll have coffee there."

When Nancy, flanked by Peter and Dick, entered the drawing room, Cynthia was looking around not as though she were admiring but as though she were shrewdly appraising the value of its contents.

She wore a black suit, the skirt so short that it startled Nancy, and the tiny red hat she had worn at the Museum. For a moment Nancy thought, with an odd pang: I'd forgotten how pretty she is.

As Cynthia turned toward the door her expression changed. She looked at Nancy, at the orange dress, at the fabulous necklace. She doesn't recognize the zombie, Nancy thought, and held back a giggle. The blue eyes moved from Peter to Dick back to Peter.

"Hello, my sweet! I didn't know you had guests."

"Nancy," Peter said, his hand warm on her bare arm as he led her toward the uninvited guest, "this is Miss Barbee. My wife, Cynthia. And let me introduce an old friend, Richard Stowell."

"Your wife!" Cynthia stood as though she had been turned to stone.

It was Dick Stowell who came to the rescue. "So you are Cynthia! I've seen that portrait Peter did of you. I thought it was terrific, but I realize now it didn't do you justice, though he told me you were the best model he ever had."

"Model." Cynthia repeated the word, looking almost stupid with shock.

"How do you do, Miss Barbee." Nancy held out her hand. "How courageous of you to look us up on such a bitterly cold night. Or perhaps, like Peter and me," and she smiled up at the tall, frozen man beside her, "you love New England winters."

Murch brought in the coffee tray and placed it before Nancy.

"Black?" Nancy asked. "Sugar?"

"Black, please. No sugar." Cynthia, Nancy thought without pity, was like an actor who was reading a part and had lost his place.

Dick carried the fragile cup to Cynthia. She started to

lift it, became aware that her shaking hands betrayed her, and set it carefully on its saucer.

"I suppose you're staying at the inn," Peter said, breaking a silence that threatened to become awkward.

"My suitcases are here." Cynthia's face hardened, a strident, challenging note came into her voice. "I didn't know——"

"Of course," Nancy broke in hastily, "our inn isn't very well known. However, it's good. Peter can make a reservation for you in the morning. But we'd be delighted to put you up tonight."

"Planning to be here long, Miss Barbee?" Dick asked.

For the first time she really noticed him, summing him up, a big man with virile good looks and a cheerful manner.

"I don't really know." The blue eyes flicked to Peter's face on which there was no expression at all. "It depends on some business affairs." Her eyes rested on the diamond necklace and she drew a long breath.

"When you're not engaged in business," Dick said, "you might brighten the hours of an old bachelor."

Cynthia laughed, the gay tinkling laugh that had once so bewitched Peter. She held out a small hand. "How kind of you! How very kind. Perhaps I'll take you up on that."

"Now you've made my day," Dick declared.

II

That night it seemed to Peter that his friend would never leave. He was on tenterhooks for fear Cynthia would make some comment about his hasty marriage, about his mysterious determination to stay in Simonton. As a rule, Dick was sensitive to atmosphere but tonight, apparently because he was greatly attracted to Cynthia, he stayed on and on, drawing her out about herself, teasing her about her secret business affairs in the village.

When he finally, and reluctantly, took his leave, he held Cynthia's hand unnecessarily long. "All Simonton needed was glamour. Now it has it. A beautiful bride and a beautiful model."

And if he could have made a more unfortunate comment, Nancy couldn't imagine what it would have been.

And at last the three were alone. Nancy, her orange dress brilliant against the corn-colored satin of her chair, sat poised and quiet. Peter leaned against the mantel. Cynthia, who had discarded her hat, curled up on a sofa of soft green velvet. She was making herself very much at home.

After looking from one to the other, Nancy got up. "You must be tired, Miss Barbee. I'll show you your room."

"Don't bother," Cynthia told her. "I want to have a talk with—your husband."

"Of course," Nancy said courteously. "Good night."

"I won't be long, dearest," Peter called after her.

There was silence in the beautiful drawing room until Nancy had reached the top of the stairs. Then Cynthia was on her feet. Her small hands clutched at Peter's arm. On one of them he saw the engagement ring he had given her.

"Who is that woman?"

"She is my wife."

"Why did you marry her?"

"Why," he countered, "have you come here? I thought you hated New England in the winter."

"I came to you because you didn't—"

"Crawl back," he suggested.

She looked at him quickly. To her surprise he wasn't angry; he was smiling. She changed her tactics. Her mouth quivered. "Oh, Peter! Darling Peter! I thought you loved me."

"I thought so, too. We both seem to have been mistaken."

"I don't believe it. Not for a minute. You were crazy about me. You still are. And I was—unreasonable. I know that. So then you just picked up this girl on the rebound. But just because we've both made mistakes we don't have to suffer forever. Get rid of her. Pay her off."

"That's enough, Cynthia." There was a note in his voice she had never heard before. "I cannot permit you to speak of my wife in those terms. Now I'll show you your room and in the morning—I suggest you return to New York."

They watched each other steadily. "I'm not going back to New York tomorrow, Peter. I'm not going until this thing is settled."

He shrugged wearily. "Look here, Cynthia, you are the one who broke our engagement. Now I am married. It is all over. There is no business for us to discuss."

"Something queer is going on," Cynthia said. "Something very queer. You gave up your diplomatic job. You gave me up to come here. And you passed me off as a—a model."

He reached automatically for his pipe, remembered that he had broken it. "Well?" he said, a note of impatience in his voice. Odd that he should be impatient with Cynthia, want nothing so much as to have her go away. At least, he realized in relief, her influence over him was gone. As he looked down, he saw her cover her big engagement ring as though to protect it.

"You needn't worry," he told her. "You can keep it. A memory of a bad investment."

She was silent, twisting the ring on her finger. When she looked up at him he was startled by the cold calculation in her eyes.

"You are up to something, Peter, my sweet. It scared you to have your attractive friend Stowell ask questions, didn't it? Well, I've got some questions to ask." She added bluntly, "Just how much would it be worth to you to have me forget those questions, Peter?"

He did not hesitate. "Not a penny. Don't believe for a single minute that I can be blackmailed. I'm warning you, Cynthia."

"Suppose," she suggested, "I smother my curiosity and go away—and take that diamond necklace with me." Something in his face made her suddenly afraid. She took an involuntary step backward.

"You'll take nothing with you. That's final."

"Then," she said, "I'll stay in Simonton until I find the answers to my questions." Seeing his expression she laughed. "And this time, my sweet, I am warning you."

III

Nancy had removed the necklace and the orange evening dress. In white silk pajamas and a robe of crimson velvet with matching slippers, she sat before the great triple mirrors, brushing her hair with long rhythmic strokes.

Her mind was in a turmoil. She had left, had practically been forced to leave, Peter and Cynthia alone. What was happening downstairs? She remembered Peter's despairing appeal, *What can I do, Nancy?* But there was nothing she could do to help. Peter would have to deal with Cynthia himself. If he still loved her—Nancy was aware of a feeling of contempt for him. How could he be taken in by that coldblooded girl? And yet Dick Stowell, too, had been immensely attracted to her. Gentlemen were supposed to prefer blondes. Poor Dick, blundering along to ease the situation and simply making things worse. Cynthia had not liked being referred to as a model. She had not liked that at all. Someone would be made to pay for that.

Nancy hoped that it would not be Peter. He had been hurt enough. But perhaps a man valued a woman the more because she had the power to hurt him. Perhaps he saw her as the unattainable dream. But Cynthia wasn't unattainable, of course. When this marriage was annulled, Peter would be free to marry her if he chose to do so. Perhaps, in a few months, when his mysterious task had been accomplished, he would marry her. When summer came, and the roses that Mrs. Henning said were so beautiful had reached their full glory, Cynthia would occupy these rooms.

In the mirror Nancy saw reflected the bedroom with its high headboard of tufted lime satin, the beige wall-to-wall carpet that was so thick one seemed to walk on a cloud, the white satin chairs, the bedside table with its telephone and small radio, the low cases crammed with the books Peter's mother had loved.

Curious how quickly she had come to feel at home in

this suite, to feel that she belonged here. And Cynthia
didn't belong here. She belonged in some noisy night spot,
not in this gracious quiet home.

But I don't belong here either, Nancy reminded herself.
I don't belong anywhere. Her reflection blurred in the
mirror and she blinked back tears. I'm ashamed of you,
she told herself. Absolutely disgusted. You've done this
for Noah, remember? Then why are you acting like this,
as though you wanted something more?

There was a light tap on the door and Peter came in. For
a moment he hesitated in the sitting room and then, seeing
her at the mirror, the black cloud of hair spilling over the
crimson robe, he caught his breath sharply. He came
slowly into the bedroom. Their eyes met in the mirror,
Nancy put down the brush and turned to face him, her
heart giving great sickening jolts.

What was Peter doing in her room? Then she remembered his bitter words, *Married bliss,* of course. He was
carrying on the game for Cynthia's benefit.

"What—what is it?" For some reason she had difficulty
in steadying her voice.

"She is going to stay, Nancy!"

"Here, you mean?"

"No, at the inn. That, at least, I can insist on."

Why? The word trembled on Nancy's lips but she did
not speak. Then she saw his expression. He looked half
angry, half dismayed, and for the first time he seemed
helpless, at a loss.

She picked up the diamond necklace from her dressing
table and held it out to him. "Please take care of this."
Then she got up and led the way to her little sitting room,
looking to see that the door to the corridor was closed.

"Do you want to tell me about it?" she asked quietly.

"I wish I could. I wish to God I could!" There was
appeal in his eyes. "It's not my secret, Nancy."

She looked down at the band of her wedding ring.
"You asked me for trust, Peter. You needn't tell me
anything. But I can't help you if I don't understand."

"At least," he said, "I can tell you about Cynthia. She
didn't believe I was through with her. She came here to
renew our engagement."

"And found you married."

"And found me married," Peter agreed.

Nancy forced herself to say quietly, "Couldn't you explain to her that this isn't—that we aren't—that eventually you will be free to marry her?"

"I didn't want to. Cynthia isn't interested in anything but the Gerard money. If I hadn't been a fool I'd have realized that long ago. And I'm not interested in Cynthia. I made that clear. Crystal clear."

"Then why is she planning to stay in Simonton?"

"Because," Peter said bluntly, "she wants to know what I am doing here, what's behind our hasty marriage. She intends to find out."

"Will that do any harm?"

"I don't know," he admitted. "There's not a chance in a million that she could stumble on—uh—the real facts. But by dropping hints, she could do a lot of damage and lessen any good that I could possibly accomplish."

"And you can't stop her?"

Peter laughed mirthlessly. "For a price."

Nancy leaned forward. "Wouldn't it be better to give her what she wants, Peter?"

Unconsciously his fingers closed over the diamond necklace in his pocket. "Only a fool would let himself be blackmailed, Nancy."

"But—"

"What trust can be put in a blackmailer? Would that silence Cynthia in the long run, particularly if she should find a—better market?"

"Could she?"

Peter thought about it. "There's always a chance, slim, but still a chance. And there's a lot at stake. But we'll fight it out with our own weapons. After all, we're the challenged party."

"What else is worrying you?"

"Dick," he admitted. "He fell for Cynthia and she knows it. I'd hate to see him entangled with that little gold digger."

Nancy smiled gently to herself. Only a week ago, Peter had been entangled and he hadn't seemed to mind. Not until he had found out what Cynthia was really like.

"Dick's a sensible person and he's levelheaded. He'll be all right."

"Perhaps." Peter was not convinced. "I wish now I hadn't told that fool lie about Cynthia being a model. She didn't like that, and if she unburdens her griefs on Dick's sympathetic shoulder—"

"He's your friend," Nancy reminded him. "Your best friend, you said. In that case, he'll never be disloyal to you, whatever she may tell him. Oh, there's one more thing; we'll simply have to ask Cynthia to the open house; there's no way out of it."

"I suppose so. But how are we going to muzzle her? I simply can't afford to have her arousing any suspicions about our staying in Simonton this winter."

"I'll see that she is kept much too busy to make trouble."

Peter smiled at her. "You're quite a girl, Nancy."

She nodded. "They call me Old Reliable."

ELEVEN

THE DAY of the open house was cold and clear. Tree trunks cast blue shadows on the sparkling snow and the sun turned it to a kaleidoscope of color that made diamonds seem dingy. A good omen, Nancy thought, as she tackled her breakfast tray with a healthy appetite.

Mr. Gerard, she was told, had been up for hours and he was working in his studio. He had left word that he was not to be disturbed. Apparently Miss Barbee was still sleeping as she had not rung for her tray.

When she had bathed and dressed in a knitted wool dress of soft heather, Nancy talked for a few moments over the telephone to Noah.

"How are the exercises going?"

He grunted a reply, which meant that he was in one of his brooding, discouraged moods.

"And the memory?"

"Don't keep nagging," he said irritably. "I'm all washed up and we both know it. Why can't you let me alone?"

"All right," she said cheerfully. "I'll let you alone all day. I'm busy with the party and, besides, we have a houseguest."

Something in her voice made him demand, "Who's that?"

"An old friend of Peter's. Don't worry. I'm not going to ask you to meet her."

"I should hope not." Noah added, "Her?"

When Nancy made no comment he said, half jokingly, "Did you say an old friend or an old flame?"

"Oh, what difference does it make?" For the first time she hung up on Noah in a bad temper.

Mrs. Henning was waiting in the morning room. "Murch said a Miss Barbee came last night and Hannah forgot to write down the message and deliver it."

"It wasn't important," Nancy said.

"It shouldn't have happened and it won't happen again," Mrs. Henning declared. "We were most distressed about it. I understand Miss Barbee is in the west room. I hope everything was all right."

"Under your painstaking supervision I am sure it was." As Mrs. Henning beamed at this tribute, Nancy went on, "Miss Barbee arrived unexpectedly and she'll be leaving after the party. Perhaps you'll have a maid pack her luggage and Max can take it to the inn. Mr. Gerard has made a reservation for her. Now about flowers—"

It was lunchtime when Nancy had occasion to speak either to Peter or to Cynthia Barbee. All morning, Peter had remained secluded, or barricaded, in his studio. Now and then, Nancy caught sight of Cynthia prowling from room to room. Once she even saw her close a drawer hastily when she was aware that she was being observed. For a while she stood watching while a buffet was set up in the formal dining room: chafing dishes waiting for the creamed crabmeat and mushrooms that would be served in pâté shells, the usual ham and turkey, paper-thin sandwiches wrapped in damp napkins to keep them fresh, anchovies and caviar, big green and ripe olives.

"Quite a spread," she remarked laconically when Peter appeared and they went into the smaller, more intimate, dining room. "Enough to feed a regiment."

"There will probably be enough left to feed one," Peter commented. "Mrs. Henning must have planned for the usual number, and this winter most of our friends and neighbors are away. There probably won't be more than two dozen guests, but I wanted them to know my wife as soon as possible."

"So she's a stranger here too." Cynthia looked from one to the other. "How did you meet each other?"

"It's too long a story to tell now."

"Too long or too improbable?" Cynthia stopped abruptly, remembering the servants in the room. "What time is this shindig?"

"Three to six," Nancy told her.

"I'm looking forward to it." Cynthia's pink tongue licked out over her lips. "I'm really looking forward to it." For a moment she watched Peter's scowling face with mocking amusement. "I can't wait to have people ask me about my life as a model."

"Have fun," Peter said savagely and caught Nancy's warning eyes. They finished lunch in silence.

When Nancy had changed to the white wool dress, she was clasping a necklace of matching pearls around her neck just as Helen came in.

"How lovely," Helen said. She had insisted on helping Nancy dress, largely, Nancy suspected, to postpone as long as possible the ordeal of meeting Noah. "The diamonds are more spectacular, of course, but these are perfect. Like moonlight. Like a dream."

"I've always loved them." Nancy paused for a final look in the mirror.

"I meant to come earlier and help you, but your guest, Miss Barbee, asked for a maid."

"I'm sorry, Helen. I told Mrs. Henning you were not to be regarded as a maid, that you were my secretary."

"I know, but the—young lady—was making such a fuss. I packed her suitcases. She brought three of them and the stuff was scattered all over the room as though she had planned to stay. I left word for Max to pick them up." Even through the disfiguring colored lenses Nancy could see the angry gleam in Helen's eyes.

"She wasn't rude to you, surely!"

Helen giggled. "She didn't seem to know I was human. 'Give me this . . . Do that . . . Don't be so clumsy.'"

"I'm sorry," Nancy said again.

"It didn't matter. All I wanted was to help keep the peace. Except when she tried to act as though she owned this place—or expected to own it." There was a scarcely veiled warning in her voice which Nancy ignored.

"She's wearing an emerald green dress that makes her

look sallow," there was satisfaction in Helen's voice, "and a skirt cut up to here." She demonstrated. "She asked what you were wearing. I said white because it was so wonderful with your hair and coloring, and very plain, of course, because, as one of the ten best-dressed women—"

Nancy gurgled with laughter. "Helen, you didn't!"

"Yes, I did," Helen said defiantly. "You look out for that girl, Mrs. Gerard. She's a troublemaker from way back or I miss my guess. From the way she was fixing herself up she's loaded for bear. Not that anyone would look twice at her when you are around."

Perhaps, Nancy thought, an hour later, it would have been better if Helen had proved to be wrong. As the wife of Peter Gerard, Nancy was warmly welcomed and the center of attention. Cynthia, after a few courteous comments, was passed by. For the first time in her life she was a background figure while the attention and admiration she usually took for granted were lavished on Peter's unexpected wife.

People came and went, shook hands with Nancy and congratulated Peter. They welcomed his lovely young wife to Simonton, accepted her as one of them. And always Peter stood protectively at her side, performing introductions, smiling, looking proud. No one seeing him would have suspected that he was not the happy bridegroom he claimed to be.

Once Nancy caught sight of them in a long narrow Venetian mirror, Mr. and Mrs. Peter Gerard, Peter looking like his great-grandfather's portrait; Nancy with such a glow of excitement in the pure oval of her face that she seemed less than ever like a madonna, the resemblance he had first recognized. For a moment Peter met her eyes in the mirror, they turned questioningly to the pearl necklace, but he said nothing.

"How lovely you are!" exclaimed a gentle voice.

"Mr. and Mrs. Wheeler, darling," Peter said. "They aren't just inhabitants of Simonton; they practically are Simonton."

"I meant to call on you as soon as you arrived but I had a slight cold and my husband insisted that I stay home. Today, of course, I had to come to welcome Peter's wife."

"You are very kind," Nancy said. For an hour she had been repeating to gracious people, "You are very kind." What would they think when they learned, as they must eventually, that her position had been a sham?

"I wish," Mr. Wheeler said to Peter, "your mother could have known your wife. She would have been so happy today."

As though he had never really looked at her before, Peter's eyes examined his wife curiously. "Yes," he agreed, "she would."

"We want you to like Simonton," Mrs. Wheeler said. "There are some fascinating old places here. That is, if you are interested in historical spots."

Nancy smiled. "Most of my historical spots have been in England and France. And Greece, of course."

There was a jovial laugh. "The Parthenon makes our little historical spots seem like upstarts."

There was an annoyed flush on Mrs. Wheeler's face and Peter said quickly, "Darling, I want you to know Mr. and Mrs. Morton."

Morton was a man in his middle sixties, a shade over-weight, a shade too well-dressed, a shade too important. His manner was better suited to a platform or a convention than to a small gathering of neighbors.

He crushed Nancy's hand, then he gave her a smacking kiss. "Always kiss the bride," he said genially.

Like her husband, Mrs. Morton was rather overweight. She was tightly corseted, wearing a black Dior dress and a large pin made of a cluster of diamonds. She wafted Chanel Number Five. Her hair had a blue rinse and was carefully done. Her face had been made up meticulously and discreetly. But, for all the array of rings on her fingers, her handclasp was warm and her manner was pleasant and unassuming. Everything that dressmakers could do had been done to make her a sophisticated woman of the world, and nothing had altered the essential directness and simplicity of her nature.

"How nice it's going to be to have someone young and pretty here," she said with a ring of sincerity in her voice.

"Sometimes I think there are too many old people. We need more youth."

"Young people go where there's life," her husband remarked. "Nothing for them here. No future; just the past."

His wife, seeing the Wheelers' annoyance, looked at him placatingly and then turned to the young man who hovered uncertainly at her side.

"Mrs. Gerard, this is Philip Miller who has settled here to do some painting. Mrs. Gerard, Mr. Miller."

The painter was tall and thin, with fine eyes, an indeterminate nose, and the lower part of his face concealed by a rather scraggly beard.

While they were exchanging greetings, Dick Stowell appeared. "Two artists in our village at one time. You ought to hold a joint exhibit."

"Two?" Miller said in surprise.

"Yes, Gerard paints. Didn't you know?"

"I had no idea. Sometime I'd like to see your work, if I may, Mr. Gerard."

"There's not much on hand right now," Peter told him, "but I am hoping to get a lot of work done this winter."

"And a model available, too," Dick went on eagerly. He looked around, found Cynthia standing alone, a sulky expression on her face, and brought her to join the group.

"Glad to see you, Hacker," Peter said, drawing Nancy away.

Hacker shook hands, beaming. "You," he told Nancy, "are a little miracle worker. My wife can hardly wait to get started house-hunting. That's awfully kind of you."

"I'm being kind to myself," she assured him.

"If I can ever do anything for you, like giving you my right arm, speak out. It hasn't been easy for Alice sitting around idle in the inn and she'll be a lot happier when she has a home of her own."

"Any woman would be," Nancy said.

"Depending, of course, on how she gets it." Cynthia had joined them so unexpectedly that Nancy was taken aback.

Hacker summed her up coolly from the blond curls to

the spike heels. He was not impressed. "Speaking for my wife, anything she gets she has more than earned."

"But I wasn't speaking—"

"How nice of you to come, Dr. Ferrell." Nancy turned to the doctor in relief. She felt as though she were holding a hand grenade, expecting it to explode at any moment. Helen had been right. Cynthia was ripe for trouble.

Nancy looked around. "I don't need to ask whether you know everybody. When I think of how lucky we are, finding a doctor like you—"

Dr. Ferrell, who had been ill at ease, not only at making his first social appearance on the avenue but at facing Nancy who had given him a dressing down he had not forgotten, expanded before her warmth and her obvious gratitude.

"Where's Helen?"

"Helen, like the angel she is, promised to spend the afternoon with my brother."

"How is your brother, Nancy?" Stowell asked.

"I refer you to Dr. Ferrell," she said gaily. "He's an expert."

"At this point," Ferrell said, "it's not a doctor Mr. Jones needs most; it's to be shaken out of his—apathy."

"But I didn't even know you had a brother," Cynthia gushed. "Do you keep him hidden, or something? Someone ought to write a story about him. The mystery of the unseen brother."

Seeing the spots of color in Nancy's cheeks, Hacker broke in quickly. "At this point, we don't need more mysteries in Simonton. We need fewer of them."

"Don't tell me there are mysteries in this one-horse village," the painter said with a laugh. Then he caught sight of Cynthia. "We-ell, where have you been hiding?" Adroitly he cut her out of the pack, steered her toward the dining room buffet.

"Hey," Stowell called in protest, "no poaching. I saw her first."

Cynthia, with two young men vying for her attention, linked an arm with each, laughing from face to face.

Nancy and Peter exchanged a look of mutual congratulation and relief. The party was going well and Cynthia was too occupied in fanning the rivalry between her admirers to do any further damage.

Talk flowed easily. For the most part these were old friends with a community of interests. As she moved from group to group, Nancy caught snatches of talk.

"What's the big news you are going to break this week, Hacker?" Morton asked in his jovial voice, in which there was an edge of mockery.

"I'm still digging for it." The editor sounded somber and again Nancy saw the expression with which he regarded Peter.

"You may be right," Wheeler was saying courteously to one of the guests, "but I am becoming increasingly uneasy. The number of malcontents is increasing daily all over the country."

"What would you do? Gag them?"

Wheeler was not amused by this flippancy. "That's not the American way. But I would expose them, find out who is backing them."

Seeing that Peter had joined the group, Nancy was preparing to move on to the next when Wheeler added, "But first I'd like to know who tells them all what to think, and follow the same line like sheep. Like the Communists. You know that phrase of theirs when anyone disagrees: 'You aren't politically mature.' Mature! And their own governments don't think they are fit to vote except the way they are told! When people start using the same phrases—" He was becoming heated.

"Oh, look here, Wheeler," Morton protested, "you act as though nothing had changed since the American Revolution."

Mrs. Morton and Mrs. Hacker were talking with the rather stilted politeness of people who have never met, who grope for common interests.

". . . all I miss here," Mrs. Morton was saying.

"I can't say I miss the theater. What I miss is a chance to do some cooking and run my own house. I never cared much for plays."

"I did. And what I miss most is that glamorous Carrington," Mrs. Morton said. "No one was ever like him. A woman's dream come true. And then he just—vanished."

She started. "What—oh, that lovely vase! I was just admiring it. What a pity."

At Nancy's signal Murch came to gather up the pieces. "I must have knocked against it," she said, and saw Peter giving her a speculative look.

A cold draft stirred the draperies in the formal drawing room as the outside door was flung open. Helen ran into the room.

"Quick!" she cried. "There's a prowler outside the guest-house."

Dick Stowell came hastily from the dining room. "What's that? I'd better take a look."

Peter turned from the group with whom he had been talking. "Everything is under control." He sounded completely unconcerned.

Nancy, who had looked from the distraught Helen to the imperturbable Peter, saw Hacker's eyes watching his host. Watching.

TWELVE

THE TAP on the door of the guesthouse was so faint that it was barely audible. There was nothing encouraging about the voice that called irritably, "What do you want?"

Helen Ferrell opened the door and closed it behind her. The man in the black and silver dressing gown did not look up. "What do you want?" he repeated. When there was no reply, he snapped, "If you haven't anything to say, get out."

"I can't get out."

Noah turned around at the sound of those helpless, trapped words, and looked at the drab girl in the big yellow glasses. She looked back at him, pressed hard against the door.

When she spoke at last her voice was shaking. "Mrs. Gerard told me to come as a substitute for Max. I didn't want to."

"You don't have to do what Nancy says. Get out and leave me alone."

"Yes, I do have to," the meek voice said, "She took me in and made a friend of me and she got my father to be your doctor and she asked him to the party today, and we've never been on the avenue before."

"So you are Dr. Ferrell's daughter."

"Yes."

"Did he tell you about me?"

She shook her head.

112

"Who did? Nancy? What did she say?"

"That you'd fight me tooth and nail. That you'd hate it."

The wool scarf slipped off her hair, pulling down the yellow glasses. Behind them were eyes the color of violets, black-fringed. They looked at him, curiously defenseless, completely frightened, but without any trace of shock at his scarred face.

"Well!" Noah Jones said. "Well, well. Did Nancy tell you about this?" He touched his face.

The incredible violet eyes studied him solemnly. "Oh, you mean the scars."

"Certainly I mean the scars." His voice rose raggedly. "What else would I mean?"

Mouse, Mrs. Gerard had called her. Helen tried to find an adequate retort.

"What else?" he repeated.

"You're not the only person in the world," Helen said, feeling like a Pekingese defying a St. Bernard. "Mrs. Gerard has other things to think of. More important things."

"Oh." He sounded rather deflated. Nonetheless, it was a relief to know that this idiotic girl wasn't upset by his appearance. She wasn't interested enough to care one way or another.

"What does your father say about me?"

"I haven't talked to him. He doesn't like me much so I ran away from home. All I know is what Mrs. Gerard said, that your recovery is up to you."

"So it's up to me. Well, if we're stuck with each other, we're stuck with each other. Sit down."

Helen took off her coat, sat on the edge of a chair, looking as though she were prepared for flight. She shoved on the unsightly glasses again.

"Take those things off," Noah told her. "They are awful."

"I—I like them."

Unexpectedly he smiled. "You have queer tastes. Why aren't you at the party?"

"I'm shy with people and they never notice me so I don't know what to do."

Noah glowered at her, watching her cower in her chair. "Look, Cinderella, why don't you wipe off those cinders? What are you afraid of?"

"Y-you."

"The scars?"

"No!" she cried, horrified. "Of course not. They don't really make any difference. Only you're so—"

"So what?"

"You're so violent."

He leaned back in his chair, shouting with laughter. When he recovered he said, "What's your name?"

"Helen."

"Helen." The scars didn't make any difference, eh? It didn't matter what he looked like. She wouldn't want to be with him in any case. "Helen," he snarled. "*Was* this the face that launched a thousand ships?"

"I think you're beastly. I thought you were just someone sick I was to look after for an afternoon, but you're cruel."

"Very sad. You break my heart. Look here, lady. I'm not the one who needs help. You are. Go take a look at yourself in the mirror. For heaven's sake, woman, fix yourself up."

"I don't know how."

"We'll start with those glasses. Give them to me. And why any sane woman would want to hide eyes like yours is beyond me. Next I'm going to teach you to stand and sit down and walk. You carry yourself like a badly packed sack of meal."

"You—"

"Stand up."

Helen stood up.

"Head high, not as though you were trying to crouch behind the chair. Now—"

After what seemed to be hours, Noah said, "All right! All right! You can sit down now. Not like that. Don't you remember anything I've been telling you?"

"I can't do one more thing. I can't move."

"You'll do as you are told," he informed her.

Helen was goaded beyond endurance. "If you think it's so important to walk," she fumed, "why don't you try it

for yourself, instead of just sitting here, like a, like a sack
of meal?"

The vitality that had filled him seemed to drain out like
sands from an hourglass. "What's the use?"

"I guess I was mistaken about you. I thought you'd be
more like your sister, that you could take anything with—
with courage. And you haven't any more than I have.
Why, you haven't as much."

There was a long silence in the room. Then Noah said,
"Stop shaking, you idiot girl! I'm not angry."

"You—aren't?"

"What's that about Nancy's courage? What need has a
happy bride on her honeymoon—"

"I was thinking of Miss Barbee."

"Who's that?"

"She came yesterday. She's an old friend of Mr.
Gerard's and there was some mistake about her message.
Everyone was upset by her coming. And she didn't even
know Mr. Gerard was married. She's very pretty but I
don't like her at all. She acts as though the house should
be hers. I wish she hadn't come. Mrs. Gerard has been so
kind to me, I don't want her to be hurt."

"You think Nancy will be hurt?"

"At least, she'd never let anyone guess." Helen broke
off abruptly.

"What is it?"

Helen had been looking out of the window. "There's
someone outside the guesthouse. When he saw me he
jumped out of sight around that clump of bushes. He's
crouching now. I think he's trying to keep out of sight of
the windows from the main house, too."

"Where's Max?"

"He's parking the cars for the party. Everyone is busy
and they may not be watching for telephone calls so I'd
better go myself."

"Stay here, you little fool! You may be running into
trouble."

"Someone has to do it." Helen caught up her coat,
ignored his protests, ran along the path Max had dug
through the snow, up the front steps, flung open the door
of the main house. There were voices and laughter from

the drawing room, the faint ring of crystal and silver from the dining room.

"Quick!" she cried. "There's a prowler outside the guest-house."

I

Cynthia did not leave until after dinner, and then only under protest. Her bags had been packed by Helen but by the time she had finished, Max was busy with the party. Later, when Cynthia learned that her suitcases were to be removed to the inn, she stormed down the stairs in search of Peter.

Already traces of the party were being deftly removed. There was no one except the servants on the lower floor. For a long time Cynthia stood at a window in the morning room looking out at the light streaming from the guest-house.

There was something very odd about Nancy Gerard's mysterious brother, the man nobody saw, the man who was being, apparently, spied upon. And Peter had not been surprised at the presence of a prowler. Not at all.

Peter. In the past twenty-four hours Cynthia had had to revise her ideas about him. She had taken him for granted, taken his devotion for granted. It had never occurred to her that she could lose him, no matter what she did. Lose the Gerard money. Not until she had entered this house and met his neighbors had she fully grasped the extent of Peter's wealth or had any inkling of his social prestige.

Her small hands clenched, beat on the windowsill. She would never again have such an opportunity. She wasn't going to lose Peter. But she had lost him, she realized. How was it possible? He had been crazy about her. And then he had married another girl. There was something in his face she could not mistake. Her influence was gone, wiped out as though it had never been.

And the other girl? Cynthia thought about Nancy Gerard. All right, she told herself frankly, the girl is beautiful. She knows how to receive people, how to talk to them easily. But Peter couldn't be in love with her. No man could change like that within twenty-four hours. So?

So, she decided, there is something wrong here in Simonton. Wrong about the marriage. Wrong with the man hiding out in the guesthouse. Wrong with Peter being here at all.

She had picked up a good deal of perplexing information from Dick Stowell. Now that was an attractive man! She could really go for a man like that. Some life to him, and he had liked her. Liked her a lot.

There was nothing romantic about Cynthia's musings, in spite of the attraction Dick Stowell had for her. Attraction was all very well but not the important thing. According to Stowell, Peter had sacrificed his diplomatic career because Nancy's brother needed seclusion and care. But that couldn't be true. Peter had planned to come here while he was still engaged to Cynthia. His reason had to be important enough for him to risk losing her.

Cynthia's eyes fell on her diamond engagement ring. When Peter had slipped it on her finger she had been exultant, feeling that she had achieved the goal of her life. But now she remembered Nancy's diamond necklace. Her face hardened.

Someone was moving around in the library. She went in to find Peter methodically filling a pipe from the rack on a smoking stand. He had changed to a dinner jacket.

He looked at her in surprise and without pleasure. "I thought you had gone. I made a reservation for you at the inn and asked Max to deliver your luggage and take you when you were ready."

"I got your message but you haven't got mine. I have news for you. I haven't gone. I'm not going."

"Oh, yes," Peter said quietly, "you are going. It will be too late now for dinner at the inn. But after dinner you are leaving this house, Cynthia, if I have to carry you."

There was a queer little smile on her lips. "Are you sure that is wise, my sweet?"

"What do you mean by that?"

"I learned a lot this afternoon from your friend Stowell. A lot of mighty interesting things. What's behind this marriage of yours, Peter?"

"That doesn't concern you."

"I just might make it my business.

"What does that mean?"

"For one thing, you're telling people here that the reason you've given up your diplomatic career was because of your brother-in-law. I happen to know you planned to come here before you had a brother-in-law. So something is wrong."

He made no comment.

"Next, someone is staking out the guesthouse. I wonder why. Before I get through, a lot of people are going to wonder why."

He relighted the pipe which had gone out. "So?" he asked when it was burning satisfactorily.

"So something is going on. Something important. Something big. Do you want me to ask questions or do you want me to keep still?"

"Suit yourself."

She watched him for a moment, saw him watching her. They were like two duelists. She smiled.

"You told your friend Stowell I was your model. Suppose I tell him I'm the girl you jilted."

"That isn't true and you know it."

"Would that matter?" Her laugh rang out mockingly in the library.

"What do you want, Cynthia?" he asked at last.

"That diamond necklace."

He rang the bell. When Murch appeared he said, "Has Max delivered Miss Barbee's luggage to the inn? Good, then ask him to take her down after dinner, will you?" He followed the butler out of the room.

For a moment Cynthia stared after him. He had refused to be bluffed! After a quick glance at the door, she dialed a number.

When she spoke her voice was muffled, almost furtive.

"I want you to come at once . . . No, not the house, the inn. It's important . . . Don't worry, it will be worth your while."

II

In answer to Noah's urgent telephone call, Peter pulled on an overcoat and boots and went out to the guesthouse when a most uncomfortable dinner was over and Cynthia had taken her departure.

Noah was already in bed and Max was straightening up the room.

"Did you get Miss Barbee to the inn?"

Max gave him an oddly unfriendly look, quickly veiled. "Yes, sir."

"Then that's all for tonight unless Mr. Jones wants you."

Noah shook his head. "Good night, Max."

When the two men were alone they appraised each other carefully.

"Anything wrong?" Peter asked, shrugging out of his overcoat.

"A hell of a lot seems to be wrong," Noah told him bluntly. "I think it's time you put me in the picture."

"What do you mean?"

"Don't play for time and don't stall!" Noah was neither in his depressed mood nor in his irritable mood. He was coldly angry. "Twice people have prowled around this guesthouse. Why?" When Peter made no reply he said, "It seems to me that I have a right to know."

"Unfortunately, I have no right to answer your questions."

"But here I am—a sitting duck—"

"You're in no danger, Noah. None in the least. The first time it happened, someone wanted to see whether you existed. The second time, this afternoon, was different. I had my own man watching to see whether anyone would check on you."

"Why? What am I supposed to have done?"

"You," Peter told him, "are my ostensible reason for being in Simonton. Someone didn't believe it. But you won't be bothered from now on. People know Dr. Ferrell has seen you and that he is handling your case. From now on, you will be accepted at face value."

"Why do you need an excuse for spending the winter in your own house?"

Peter looked squarely at his brother-in-law. Because of the other man's disfigurement he had been cautious in the past about causing any embarrassment by staring at him. He barely knew what Noah looked like. Now he saw that the eyes searching his were like Nancy's, that the chin was strong and determined. Stubborn, perhaps. Up to now he had regarded him as a querulous invalid whose condition would be useful to him. Now he saw that he had a man, and a very angry man, to deal with.

"I can't tell you that. I can only give you my word that it's important."

"To whom?"

"To all of us, perhaps. Have a heart, man! I'm not a free agent."

"Whose agent?" Noah added, with a touch of his familiar irritability, "You aren't the only one who can keep a secret if it's that important. And God knows I'm so isolated from the human race that there is no one for me to reveal it to." He repeated insistently, "Whose agent?"

"Uncle Sam's," Peter said at last.

"And what," Noah asked, "has that girl of yours to do with Uncle Sam?"

"My girl?"

"The one Helen Ferrell told me barged in and tried to take over your house—and you. The girl who didn't know you were married. What goes on here?"

Painfully Noah pulled himself out of the chair, balanced himself against a table. "Nancy is my sister and I'm not going to have her hurt, dispossessed in her own home after less than a week of marriage. What is this girl to you, Peter? I want a straight answer."

"All right," Peter capitulated wearily. "Only, for heaven's sake, sit down before you fall down."

Noah dropped back in his chair but his eyes never left Peter's face. Slowly, awkwardly, Peter told him of his engagement to Cynthia; then he had been asked to do a job for the government and Cynthia refused to accompany him to Simonton, refused to marry him unless he would provide her with the glamorous honeymoon she wanted.

Then Nancy had appeared on the scene. She had overheard the whole conversation. Like a melodramatic fool, he had told Cynthia he would marry the first girl he met before he would crawl back to her. Then Nancy had come up to him, had said, had suggested—Peter broke off.

"So that's it," Noah said at last. "Because I refused to take any more self-sacrifice, she told me she was engaged. She did that for me. Good God! Ruined her life for a worthless brother, a mock marriage, and the humiliation of having a jeering rival at hand."

"It's not that bad," Peter assured him. "Nancy and I will have the marriage annulled as soon as my job here is done. A lot depends on it, Noah. More than your pride or Nancy's happiness or my future. A lot more than you can imagine. So far as Cynthia is concerned, I know now that she is a gold digger. She's even turned blackmailer. But I don't scare. We can fight this out if we work together and not if we work against each other. It's a good fight."

"All right," Noah agreed reluctantly. "But I wonder if any man is capable of the total kind of sacrifice a woman can make."

Peter shrugged. "That depends on the woman."

"At least," Noah suggested, "you might protect Nancy's dignity by paying a little attention to her. That can't interfere with your earthshaking secret."

"I'll remember," Peter said guiltily. Before leaving the guesthouse he paused. "Oh, there's one thing. Someone mentioned the strange disappearance of Carrington this afternoon and Nancy was so startled she knocked over a vase. Why?"

Noah looked at him blandly. "I haven't the faintest idea."

"Women are queer." Peter sounded disgruntled, bad-tempered. "I wouldn't have thought he was her type."

After the door closed, Noah sat listening to Peter's footsteps crunching over the frozen snow. A smile quirked his lips. His chest heaved. He was chuckling.

THIRTEEN

NEXT morning there was an improbably deep blue sky for February. Nancy was awakened by the rattle of covers as Helen brought in the breakfast tray and deposited it, with a sigh of relief, on the table.

"I told Mrs. Henning you aren't my maid," Nancy expostulated, as she reached for slippers and robe. "This waiting on me has got to stop."

"I came," Helen said, "because I wanted to tell you personally that I am resigning. Right now."

Nancy looked at her in surprise. Something about Helen was different. "Where are your yellow glasses?"

"Your brother took them away." The long, dark-lashed violet eyes looked at Nancy balefully. "He said, 'Was this the face that launched a thousand ships?' He said, 'Woman, fix yourself up!' He made me walk and stand and sit. He—he—he—"

Nancy rocked with laughter. "Wonderful! Let him storm. He's interested."

"He said I was an idiot girl. He—he—he—"

"I told you he needed a challenge. He's so used to women trying to be glamorous for him, trying to please him, that I knew you were just what would turn the trick, just what he needed."

"He's not what I need."

As the telephone on her bedside table rang, Nancy reached out to answer it. "Good morning, Noah . . . Some

what? . . . Why, for heaven's sake? . . . Oh, all right, I'll
order them today. Special delivery . . . And what? . . .
Look here, be reasonable. I can't order the girl . . . Well,
if she'll come, which I doubt. But I warn you right now,
she's here with me and . . . She came to resign . . . Because
you bullied her, you dope! . . . Well, I have an idea. Max
is driving for me today. I'm taking Mrs. Hacker to look at
houses . . . You wouldn't know her anyhow, the wife of
the local newspaper owner. So if you must have someone
read to you, I'll ask Helen. But strictly as a favor. And if
she refuses, you can just spend the day alone. And serve
you right."

Nancy looked at Helen, looked away again, struggling
to keep her lips straight. "I know it's lonely out there. I'm
very sorry but . . . What? Wait a minute . . . Helen says
she'll read to you for a while."

While Nancy ate her breakfast she and Helen discussed
what the latter had better read to Noah.

"Have you had much experience reading aloud?" Nancy asked casually.

"Not a bit."

Nancy turned away to hide a grin. "There's *The Oxford
Book of English Verse*," she suggested, "and that new
novel everyone is talking about and nobody seems to read,
and—are there any plays on the shelves there?"

Helen bent over to look at the books. "Shakespeare,"
she said doubtfully, "but I don't know—"

"Try *The Taming of the Shrew*. That's gay enough."

While Helen dubiously gathered the books together,
Nancy looked through her new wardrobe. For herself she
chose a wool suit of leaf green. She pulled out the heather
knit dress.

"We're the same size," she said. "Why don't you wear
this today? The color is just pale enough to make your
eyes terrific by contrast, and brown is wrong for you. It's
too drab. You need brightening up."

Helen's lips compressed. "You are beginning to sound
like your brother."

"You," and Nancy laughed impishly, "ain't seen noth-
in' yet."

"I don't know why you are doing this." Reluctantly

Helen removed the shabby, ill-fitting dress, let Nancy pull the other over her head and zip it up.

"Now," Nancy said triumphantly, "look at yourself. You have the kind of figure any woman longs for and you go around looking—"

"Like a badly packed sack of meal," Helen finished glumly. "That's what Mr. Jones said."

"Not now. And when we've done something about your hair—"

As she turned slowly before the triple mirror, a delighted smile hovered over Helen's lips. She gathered up the books. "Well, I'd better get started. I hope he's not—too cross."

"Look here, Helen, I'd better explain. Noah was in a terrible accident. His wife was killed. He was smashed up and disfigured. Because of shock and strain he has lost his memory, at least he can't retain things in his memory for more than a few minutes, though I hope that is just temporary. It's an emotional thing, and there's a good chance he will get over it. And because of all that, he can't work at his job. So if he gets irritable there's some reason for it. I don't say that's any excuse, of course. And most of that manner of his is sheer defense."

"Defense!"

"Yes, defense," Nancy told her quietly. "Nothing can convince Noah that he isn't—repellent to people, so he tries to make them believe he doesn't want them around, a kind of self-protection."

"Oh."

"Tell him I'll see him this afternoon, and I hope he'll do his exercises. He really needs to build up his resistance. And if he's impossible, throw a book at him."

I

Mrs. Hacker was waiting in the lobby of the inn, her eyes sparkling. She came forward eagerly to greet Nancy.

"I can't tell you how grateful I am."

"I've been looking forward to this excursion. Do you have a list?"

Mrs. Hacker pulled one out of her handbag. "There aren't many possibilities in our price range," she said a little doubtfully, "and some of them are old farms way out of town. But Joe says if I really like one, we can afford a second car, a small one, of course, so I could get back and forth. Naturally, we'd have to take that into account in considering the price of the house."

She consulted the list. "The first one is right across the street, the first house on the avenue. But I don't know. I hadn't thought in terms of the avenue."

"It won't hurt to try," Nancy said.

When Max stopped the car, Nancy cried out in protest. "Oh, no! They can't sell this." It was the early seventeenth-century house she had stopped to admire. "Why this should belong to the community. It must be unique."

"It's called the Maltby house and no one seems to have lived in it for two hundred years. No point even in going in," Mrs. Hacker said. "It would have to be completely rebuilt inside."

"We'll see about this," Nancy decided. "I have an idea."

They went on to the houses within the village limits and extended their range out of town. They plowed through snow to examine houses with old-fashioned plumbing, kitchens so big and inefficient a woman would walk herself to death getting a meal, small bedrooms under the eaves, with little light or air.

Nancy kept up a gay flow of talk, but as the places were scratched off, one by one, Mrs. Hacker's hopefulness dwindled. Two of the houses had been attractive, except for price. The rest were beyond redemption, even by the most willing hands, except at an impossible cost for renovation.

The last address was on a dirt road on which a single lane had been cleared, but which had not been sanded. For the first time Max, who had cheerfully cleared off snow-covered steps and negotiated unlikely roads and driveways, hesitated.

"Do you have a map?" he asked.

Nancy shook her head.

"I should have brought one. Mr. Gerard has a large-scale local map at the house."

"Is anything wrong, Max?"

"Well, this looks like a dead end to me. But if we can get in, I guess we can get out."

A quarter of a mile farther on, they came to a white picket fence, only the tops of which showed above the snow. There were double gates, and on a post the sign, FOR SALE.

"The end of the road," Max announced as he opened the door for them.

"Can you turn around?"

"The driveway has been cleared," he pointed out, unlatched the gates, and started to follow them in.

"You get the car turned around," Nancy said.

Mrs. Hacker stood still, in spite of the cold, looking at the white farmhouse, a two-story building with long windows on either side of a beautiful doorway. Behind, as with many New England farmhouses, there was a lower kitchen roof, a shed, a big stable, all attached so that men need not go out of doors in bitter weather to feed the stock.

"All that house needs," she said, "is to be lived in. And the price—why it's much lower than most of the others."

"Not much call for working farms in these parts any more," Max put in. "The soil's too rocky."

Nancy looked at him in surprise. This was the first time he had accompanied them to the house itself.

He answered her inquiring look. "Someone has been here," he explained. "No one cleared that driveway just for the exercise. The place is supposed to be unoccupied. I think Mr. Gerard would expect me to go along."

"Surely no one looking for a free night's lodging would come this far," Mrs. Hacker protested.

"You mean tramps?" Nancy asked with a shiver.

"Tramps don't usually clear driveways," Max said. He was embarrassed but determined. "If you'll let me have that key, I'll go first."

Mrs. Hacker handed it to him. After several attempts he said, "This is the wrong key."

"It can't be. Look at the tag. That's the one the real estate agent gave my husband."

Max bent over. "Someone has put a new lock on the door."

"Then we can't get in?" Mrs. Hacker could not conceal her disappointment.

Max smiled. "Not unless you want me to break a window."

"Heavens, no. But, oh dear, it seems so perfect. All I dreamed of."

"We'll get the right key and come back," Nancy told her cheerfully. "There's always another day."

As they drove back to Simonton, Mrs. Hacker said, "I can't begin to express my gratitude, even if the house proves to be unsuitable. You've opened up a whole new future for me today."

"I'm glad," Nancy said simply.

"How lucky for me that your husband should be here this winter! Joe says it has never happened before, except for fleeting visits while his mother was alive."

A cold draft seemed to have entered the warm, luxurious car. Mrs. Hacker's hands were turning and twisting her handbag over and over. She wants to tell me something, Nancy realized, and remembered Joe Hacker watching Peter, weighing him in the balance, distrusting him.

Whatever it is, I must not hurry her, must not attempt to force her confidence, Nancy warned herself. If I do that I'll destroy all we have begun to build together in the way of friendship. I must not ask anything. But, for all her resolution, a voice was crying in her mind: *What is Peter doing here?* She clenched her hands, and through her left glove she felt the pressure of her wedding ring. The ring itself might be a mockery but the trust that Peter had asked of her was real.

As the car moved slowly over a narrow bridge she saw the black water beneath, hemlocks laden with snow above.

"Oh, what a lovely world!" she cried out.

Mrs. Hacker looked at the glowing face of the girl beside her. Impulsively, she pressed Nancy's hand. "People like you will always make it lovely for others. I hope—other people will make it equally lovely for you."

Nancy said slowly, "I think you want to tell me something, Mrs. Hacker."

"No, I don't," the older woman said frankly. "It's Joe's idea. He thought I should tell you. Warn you. But the way I see it, more trouble is caused by people talking, telling things, even for the best of motives, but—" She met Nancy's steady, inquiring eyes. "Oh, it's nothing really. Only that girl, the dizzy blonde who was at your party yesterday. I didn't get her name clearly but someone said she was a model."

"Miss Barbee." Nancy's voice was steady.

"That's the one. As I suppose you know, she is staying at the inn. Came late last night and, an hour or so later, some man tapped on her door—her room's across the hall from ours—and they whispered a lot and then went down to the lobby to talk. This morning there was a new guest at the inn, a Mr. Nemeau, who sat at a different table and didn't even look at her, but I felt sure he was the same one. So did Joe. And as Joe said, 'When a man doesn't look at that girl, and when she pays no attention to a man, there's something darned strange."

Nancy laughed. "Well, after all, Miss Barbee's life is her own. It doesn't concern me."

Mrs. Hacker pulled off her gloves, straightened the kid fingers, as though the task absorbed her.

"Well, the thing is, she's concerned with you. And your husband. She has been asking questions about you both in the village, and I heard her on the telephone, agreeing to lunch with that nice Mr. Stowell."

Nancy laughed again. "I think Dick Stowell can look out for himself."

"Yes—well—"

"There's something else, isn't there?"

Mrs. Hacker looked miserable. "Joe thinks you are a fine person. I told you that before. And you have been so nice to me. He wanted—he said—" She took a long breath. "The thing is that he'd be pleased if you'd stop to see him at his office as soon as you can. Only—he said not to mention it. To anyone. Please."

II

While Nancy was looking at houses with Mrs. Hacker,
Peter had an unexpected caller. Philip Miller, in corduroy
slacks and a garish turtle-neck sweater, looked at him
rather diffidently. In spite of his beard, or perhaps because
of it, he seemed very young.

"I hope I'm not out of order," he said. "But you did
tell me I could look at your work."

"Of course," Peter agreed readily. "How about some
coffee? It's a cold morning for walking." He ordered the
coffee and led the way upstairs to his studio.

"How I envy you this light," Miller said feelingly. "And
the space. When I turn around in a hurry I knock over
furniture."

"My solution to that problem," Peter said, "was not to
have any." He waved to the room's single chair. "Make
yourself comfortable. At least as comfortable as you can
be on that thing." He lifted a canvas onto the easel. Then
a second. Then a third.

Miller said nothing until after Murch had brought in a
tray with a pot of coffee and cups and saucers. The
painter sipped coffee slowly.

At length he asked, "Have you done anything recently?"

Peter turned to the canvases stacked against the wall. "I
started this the other day." Against a dark background he
had painted Nancy's head, eyes downcast, the only light
coming from a stained glass window, so that the colors,
purple and blue, green and gold and a soft crimson,
turned the living girl into a mosaic.

"I saw her like that when we were being married."

The painter drew a long breath. "My God! I had no
idea. I thought from what Stowell said that you were an
amateur, a dabbler."

"If by that he meant I hadn't sold anything, he is right.
I have never exhibited. But painting has always been a
compulsion with me, and now at last I have time to work
at it. If I can get enough done, I'd like to have a one-man

show late in the spring. After all, I don't often take holidays, so I have to make full use of them."

"Any man who can paint like that and who does anything else is mad," Miller told him.

"There you agree with my wife. She thinks I should make it my full-time career and forget all about diplomacy."

When Miller had seen the rest of Peter's canvases he grinned ruefully. "After this, I won't dare show you my stuff. The master looking at the work of a small-town art teacher."

Peter laughed but his eyes were bright. He felt exhilarated. Miller's tribute was sincere and he felt on top of the world. Then he reminded himself that he was not in Simonton to be a painter, whatever he might say. He had another job to do.

FOURTEEN

To HELEN's relief, the hitherto irascible Mr. Jones appeared to be in a good humor. He took a long measuring look at her when she came in, wearing Nancy's dress, which fitted beautifully, her lovely eyes no longer concealed behind disfiguring colored glasses as big as goggles.

"Good morning," he said cheerfully, "it's very nice of you to come out to keep me company. Gets lonely here."

Today, he had, with Max's help, managed to dress and he was attempting to walk around the room, never out of reach of the wall or a piece of furniture on which he could lean. Back and forth. Back and forth. There was perspiration on his forehead but he kept on doggedly. Once he stumbled and caught hold of a big armchair, breathing heavily.

"Haven't you done enough?" Helen asked anxiously.

"I can't pick up strength if I don't try."

"But you shouldn't overdo it. Would it help to take my arm?"

He wiped his forehead. "You couldn't hold me up for half a minute."

"I could try."

He grinned at her. "I thought you were the girl who was afraid to try anything. Then you offer to hold up a man who is nearly twice your weight, and you dash out to face a prowler."

"He ran away. Anyhow, someone had to do it."

131

At last he dropped into the chair by the fire, leaning back in exhaustion.

"Do you want me to read to you?" she asked timidly.

"Not for the moment. Have to catch my breath first." Without opening his eyes, he asked casually, "What happened to the houseguest?"

"Miss Barbee? She went to the inn last night, thank goodness."

"Then she is staying here in town?"

"I suppose so."

"What is she up to, Helen?"

Before she could answer, there was a tap on the door and then it was flung open. Cynthia Barbee came in, the pert red hat on her blond curls, blue eyes avid and malicious as they recognized Helen.

"Oh," she said, dismissing her from her attention, "you are the maid. I was wondering whether I could do anything for Mrs. Gerard's poor brother. I know he—"

She caught sight of Noah, the sun full on his face, and drew in her breath with a hiss. One hand covered her lips. Her eyes widened. "Oh!" It was a gasp. She wheeled around and went out, not bothering to close the door behind her.

Helen saw Noah's hands tighten on the chair arms, saw his expression. She slammed the door.

"I believe," she said quietly, "I could murder that woman with my bare hands. I'd—I'd like to boil her in oil. Slowly. I'd like to see her flogged through the town at a cart the way they did to evil women in England two hundred years ago. I'd like to—"

"Stop for breath and you'll find it is easier."

She looked at him and found, in astonishment, that he was laughing. Actually laughing.

"It's all right, Kitten. You control those impulses. And what has happened to you? Yesterday you were all set to claw me. Now you're ready to protect me. Whose side are you on, anyhow?" The laughter died away. "Woman's instinct, I suppose. Protecting the weak."

"Weak! You? And, anyhow, I wasn't—and, anyhow, I came here to read to you." She showed him the books.

"Hm. I can do without that gloomy novel. It's supposed

to be so profound that even the author doesn't know what it means. And I doubt, Kitten, whether you are up to the higher flights of poetry."

"Why, you—"

"Let's try *The Taming of the Shrew*."

"I don't know whether I could read a play. I'd be afraid to try a classic."

"Classic." Noah drew a long breath. "Look here, idiot child, Shakespeare isn't a dead classic to be put on the shelves. He wrote plays, plays so wonderful that no one but the Greeks ever equalled them. Plays to be acted. Something alive. Understand?"

Helen began to read. She had gone on for some time before she looked up to see that the unpredictable Mr. Jones was shaking with laughter, trying to muffle the sounds. She faltered, went on to the next speech: "But will you woo this wildcat?" Then she glared at Noah. "What—what's so funny?"

He wiped tears from his eyes. "You with that prim, sedate little voice reading a slapstick comedy as though it were your history lesson."

"I suppose you could do better."

"One thing sure, I couldn't do worse." He took the book out of her hand and began to read. His voice rang out, flamboyant, blustering, confident, mocking:

Why came I hither but to that intent?
Think you a little din can daunt mine ears?
Have I not in my time heard lions roar?
Have I not heard the sea, puff'd up with winds,
Rage like an angry boar chafed with sweat?
Have I not heard great ordnance in the field
And heaven's artillery thunder in the skies?
Have I not in a pitched battle heard
Loud larums, neighing steeds, and trumpets' clang?
And do you tell me of a woman's tongue . . .

He read on, grandiloquent, brutal, boasting, laughing, his magnificent voice rolling out the wonderful nonsense. Then when he came to Katharina's last speech, the long one so full of assumed meekness and penitence, and behind which one senses that the shrew is still untamed, there was a glint in the violet eyes as though some new idea had struck Helen.

" 'Tis wonder, by your leave, she will be tamed so," Noah read, and closed the book.

There was a long silence in the room. Then Helen said quietly, "So that's who you are!"

The swashbuckling manner dropped away. "What do you mean?"

"You are Neil Carrington. No one else ever did Petruchio like that. Next to your Mercutio—well, perhaps your Hotspur is the best."

Noah Jones closed his eyes. "It must be time for your lunch."

"Mr. Carrington—"

"Neil Carrington is dead."

"Neil Carrington is alive. I've just heard one of his great performances." When he made no reply she asked, "Why do you call yourself Noah Jones?"

"Why not? After all, it's my name. But not quite the right one for an actor."

"When are you going back to your profession?"

"Never."

"Why?"

He lifted tired eyelids. "You're persistent, aren't you, Kitten?"

"I feel like a zoo," she said resentfully. "You call me a kitten. Your sister calls me a mouse."

"I hope she does it politely, like Alice, and addresses you as 'O mouse.' "

Helen ignored this frivolous comment. "Why aren't you?" she repeated.

"My memory isn't reliable. I couldn't remember a single speech, let alone a whole role. Besides, look at me."

"I am looking at you." The violet eyes were fixed unflinchingly on him.

"You see what my face did to the girl who barged in here."

"It's nothing," she assured him with spirit, "to what I'd like to do to her face."

"Pull in those claws, Kitten."

"When you've built up your strength and have that last bit of plastic surgery—"

"I hate nagging women," he snapped.

"I haven't much use for bad-tempered men. And don't shout at me either. 'Think you a little din can daunt mine ears?' "

He sat up abruptly. "Hey, where do you think you are going?"

"Up to the house. As you said, it's nearly time for lunch."

"When will you be back?"

Something in his dark eyes made her heart lurch. For the first time in her life she was aware of her power over a man. The eternal Eve rose, exulting and unregenerate.

"I resigned today."

"Well, you can unresign tomorrow."

"Look here, Petruchio—"

"Look here, my little shrew—"

The violet eyes were shining. Then Noah spoke and she realized, with her customary humility, that her brief moment of power was over.

"Helen," he said soberly, "tell Peter about the way that Barbee girl burst in here, will you? She didn't come to soothe the fevered brow of Nancy's brother, that's for sure. She couldn't care less about what happens to Nancy or to anyone associated with her."

"Then why did she come?"

"Let Peter find the answer to that. It seems to be a part of his job."

I

While Helen Ferrell was trudging along the snow-bordered path from the guesthouse to the main house, Dick Stowell was waiting impatiently in the inn lobby for Cynthia Barbee. In a few moments Miller came in, caught sight of him, and stopped short.

Dick laughed. "I beat you to it. She's lunching with me."

The manager, who had come out hopefully, looked at the painter's sweater and corduroy slacks and realized that he did not expect to stay for lunch. He retreated in dejection.

"I might have known. Let a pretty girl come in sight—" Miller's grumble changed. His face lighted up. "I've been looking at Gerard's paintings."

"Well?"

"They are magnificent. When he holds his one-man show he is going to be like Lord Byron who woke up to find himself famous."

"That good?"

"Dick, I'm telling you. He is going to be one of the really great ones. I was bowled over. And there was one of his wife. He'd conquered technical problems I didn't know could be solved. He made a living portrait and at the same time a kind of stained-glass effect that—"

Stowell beamed. "So he is really going to become a painter. I'm awfully glad he has salvaged something out of this marriage."

"If you had seen that portrait of his wife you'd get an idea just how much he got out of it."

High heels clicked along the lobby and Cynthia came in, wearing a black silk dress with gold ornaments, as exquisite as an old-fashioned valentine, her blond hair carefully arranged, blue eyes wide and smiling. She looked from one man to the other and her smile deepened.

"Get lost," Stowell said with a laugh, and the painter took himself off, calling, "My turn next."

Only a few tables in the dining room were occupied: Two middle-aged women, an elderly couple who were spending the winter at the inn; starry-eyed young lovers on their honeymoon; a quiet young man who was reading the *New York Times,* the Hackers at their usual corner table. Mrs. Hacker was flushed with excitement and unusually voluble; her husband was smiling sympathetically over her pleasure. Alone, at a table against the wall sat a ferret-faced young man, prematurely bald, who combined an aggressive rudeness to the waitress with a curious uncertainty toward the other diners.

Joe Hacker looked across the room as Dick held a chair for Cynthia, nodded to him, and made a low-voiced comment to his wife.

When they had ordered, Dick looked across the table at Cynthia. "And how are you filling your time in Simonton? Have you had an interesting morning?"

To his surprise the flirtatious smile faded. "It was horrible," she said, her voice just above a whisper. Whatever had happened to her, she was sincere about her feeling.

"What happened?" he asked in surprise.

"Have you seen Peter's brother-in-law? The one he keeps out of sight in the guesthouse?"

"No. Have you?"

She nodded, swallowed, reached for a glass of water. "I didn't believe he existed. I thought he was just an excuse; so I went out there. He—he's all scarred. I just took to my heels after one look."

"Good lord! That bad?"

She nodded mutely.

They had finished soup and were waiting for their main course when Dick said, "Why on earth didn't you believe Peter had a brother-in-law? I thought he said you were old friends."

"What he told you," she said with asperity, "was that I was a model. That's not true. He did a portrait of me but that doesn't make me a professional model, which is what he deliberately tried to make you believe."

"Perhaps," Dick said awkwardly, "I misunderstood him."

Cynthia was angry. "You understood just what he intended you to understand."

"But, my dear girl—"

"I hoped you would be on my side." Her voice had changed again, was soft and helpless and appealing. She dabbed carefully at the long artificial eyelashes and eyes that showed no trace of tears. Seeing her swift shift of attitude, Dick recognized in a flash the quality in her which it had taken Peter Gerard months to grasp.

"The moment I saw you," she went on, "there was something—as if there were some sort of rapport between us. I've never experienced it before."

Now what, he wondered, is the girl up to? Those cracks about her being a model had really infuriated her.

"But I am on your side," he told her earnestly. "The

thing is, Peter and I are old friends. Why on earth would he tell me something like that? Particularly about a girl like you?"

"Because he jilted me. He just—walked out on me." She saw him look at the solitaire diamond. "Yes, that's Peter's ring. And I must say he let me keep that. But the day before we were to be married he simply—threw me over. No reason at all. And I cared so much. I came up here to see if we couldn't make it all up. And he had married that girl all of a sudden. How could he do it?"

Remembering his first sight of Nancy, Dick reflected that there was no difficulty in seeing why Peter had made the choice he had; the difference between real diamonds and paste. But to break off his engagement so brutally was out of character.

"I suppose," he suggested, "you hope by staying here that you can—change things."

"I intend to try." Her eyes were as cold as marbles. "People don't change in one single day, and he was crazy about me. You can't tell me that could change overnight. I don't see why I should sit back and take it."

"Are you being wise? After all, Peter is married. You can't change that."

"Then he's got to pay for breaking my heart."

Enlightened at last, Dick sat back, looking at her steadily. "I've known Peter for a long time. He's the last man in the world to be pushed around."

She smiled at him. "We'll see." She leaned forward, fluttering her lashes. "Now tell me all about you."

FIFTEEN

AFTER Miller had left the house, Peter made a telephone call. A few minutes later he went briskly down the street. When he reached the village center he turned left and walked to a tavern that was deserted for the winter but which had an enclosed porch whose door was unlocked. Foster was already waiting for him, stamping his feet to keep warm, overcoat collar turned up around red ears.

"Is this the best you could do?" the FBI man complained.

"At least, we are out of the wind here and no one is likely to see us. That's one of the problems in a village this size. It's hard to go anywhere without being recognized."

"You're telling me," Foster said glumly. "Sorry that girl saw me yesterday afternoon. I hope it didn't make any trouble."

"None at all. Every community might have its prowlers."

"But if she sees me at the inn and recognizes me—"

"She won't. She is staying at my house and she has no social life at all."

"Who is she?"

"Daughter of the local doctor. Helen Ferrell."

"Anything new?" Foster asked. "If not, there is no point in my hanging around Simonton; now your brother-in-law's illness is established, no one is going to investigate the guesthouse."

"One thing. You remember warning me that someone might like a look at my pictures?"

"You mean it's happened already?"

"This morning. Fellow named Philip Miller. A protégé of Mrs. Morton."

"Well?"

Peter grinned. "I passed with flying colors."

"So we know Philip Miller wasted no time to check on you. That's good news. We'll look into his background. Who is this woman who is backing him?"

"She seems to be a nice simple soul. Her husband is a retired industrialist. A good deal of money, judging by the way they live."

"Native of Connecticut?"

"No, he only bought up here a year or two ago."

"Supposed to like country living?"

"I'd say he'd be the life of a party on a convention. But his wife prefers simple things."

"I'll look into Mr. Morton. He's the most hopeful candidate yet. Anything else?"

"Joe Hacker," Peter said. "Personally I like the guy. He seems all right to me."

"We checked on him after you called. You couldn't find a cleaner record, and everyone liked him. Usually there is some back-biting and jealousy when a man lands one of the big coveted prizes. Nothing like that. What seemed wrong to you?"

"To me—nothing." Peter groped for his pipe, removing his gloves so he could fill it. Foster waited patiently. He was accustomed to waiting, and Gerard was not a man to be pushed.

"Two things disturbed me, trivial, of course, but—well, the night we got here, my friend Dick Stowell dropped in. He was curious about Hacker. Said that he acts rather furtive, digs into things that don't concern him. He wondered what Hacker does all the time at his printing plant. And, of course, there's a printing plant somewhere getting out this pernicious stuff which is being distributed all over the country.

"That's all there is to it. Just a query. And my wife tells me that Hacker dislikes me." Peter grinned. "Not that there's anything out of line with that."

"Speaking of your wife," Foster said casually, "I hope that rather unusual situation is working out all right. The brother's condition is really a great help because it makes your whole story convincing."

"The real problem is," Peter said, "that my—former fiancée appeared rather unexpectedly on the scene day before yesterday. She didn't know I was married, but she does know, of course, that the whole story about Noah is a fabrication, that I planned to come here before my marriage."

"I figured something was up when I saw her name on the inn register. That girl is a potential troublemaker."

Peter looked quickly at the quiet man beside him. "How do you know?"

"When a man is asked to do a big job for the government, Uncle Sam wants to know about him. All about him. There is only one strike against you; that's the girl you were planning to marry. But you had so much else we needed that we gambled on her. And that is why there were cheers and the throwing up of hats in jubilation when you announced that the engagement was off and told us of the rather surprising suggestion of Miss Jones. That's why we urged you to go full speed ahead."

"I—see." Peter's face flushed darkly. He puffed at his pipe, finally knocked it out impatiently. "I can spare you some part of your revelations. I've already found out that Cynthia is a blackmailer. She has offered to leave Simonton in exchange for a diamond necklace, which, incidentally, is worth thirty-five thousand dollars."

"I take it you refused to play. I just saw her at the inn. Quite an eyeful. She was lunching with a big fellow, looked like an ex-football player."

"That would be my friend Stowell. And, to answer your question, yes, I refused to play." When the silence was prolonged Peter asked, "Was that a blunder? From your standpoint, I mean?"

Foster shrugged. "I'm no crystal gazer. She'll certainly do her best to find out what you are up to here. We don't know a whole lot about her. The kinds of trouble she mixes in are usually hushed up. But her brother is a different kettle of fish."

"Her brother! I thought she was an only child."

"He has a record as long as your arm. Small stuff as a rule. The sort of thing for which our kindhearted judges give suspended sentences so they can go out and do it all over again. But the law finally caught up with him and sent him away for a year. Burglary. He was released just a couple of weeks ago."

Foster stamped his feet, rubbed his ears. "Why don't I ever get an assignment in Arizona? Well, the two of them have so many aliases we don't know what their real name is. Barbee, for instance. The brother used to use a Third Avenue saloon, called the Bar B, as his informal headquarters."

"So that's why Cynthia wanted the wedding private. No disclosures until I was legally sewed up."

Foster looked at the other man but Gerard did not seem to be upset; surprised, certainly.

"Well, I have a hunch the brother has turned up here in Simonton," Foster said. "Late last night there was a lot of whispering at Miss Barbee's door and then the conference was continued downstairs. This morning there was a new guest at breakfast. He and the girl didn't look at each other, and I think he's the one. French name of Nemeau; in Latin, that's Nemo. It translates in English, as I don't need to tell you, as Nobody. If I'm right, the girl has sent for reinforcements."

Peter pinched his lower lip between his fingers, frowning.

"We'll soon know if I'm right," Foster said cheerfully. "I tipped the waitress to bring me his water glass after breakfast. Ought to pick up some nice prints."

"But won't the waitress talk?"

"If you had heard the way he ordered her around, as though she were a dog—I'll bet right now she is praying that I find something against him. She won't open her mouth. Well, you may be part Eskimo but I am half frozen. Remember, when you call me, you are Mr. Elwood and I am Mr. Perkins."

"So far," Peter pointed out amiably, "I've been able to remember that simple fact. Wait, Foster, before you hurry off. What are you holding out on?"

The FBI man expressed polite surprise. "Nothing at all."

"You checked on Cynthia Barbee's background. Are you trying to make me believe that you encouraged my marriage without checking on Anne Jones?"

"Naturally we did. You needn't worry about her. Lived abroad, went to good schools until her brother's accident. I suppose you know who he is?"

"You mean he isn't Noah Jones?"

"Oh, yes. But he is better known by his stage name. He's the Shakespearean actor, Neil Carrington."

"Well, I'll be damned!" Peter began to laugh. "But I hadn't needed any report of yours to be sure about Nancy. Old Reliable. Absolutely trustworthy."

The two men left the cold porch and walked back toward the village center. Peter gestured with his pipe toward a small red building set well back from the road.

"That's the office and printing plant of the Simonton *Weekly Gazette*."

As he spoke the door opened and a girl came out. She started toward the village center.

"That's a beauty!" Foster said.

"That's my wife," Peter told him in a queer voice.

"We had better part here. Keep in touch." Foster strolled back to the inn.

Peter followed Nancy, wondering why she had been calling on the editor. Wasn't there anyone he could trust, he wondered bleakly.

They went along the avenue, Nancy walking swiftly, Peter more slowly. Bringing up the little procession was a second man. Neither of them was aware of him.

I

The Simonton *Weekly Gazette* consisted of two rooms. The larger one at the back contained the printing press. The smaller room in front was the editorial office. It held a large, battered, unpainted desk equipped with a typewriter and goosenecked lamp, swivel chair, a metal wastebasket which appeared to be unused as the floor was ankle-deep in crumpled paper, and two cane-bottomed chairs. The desk and chairs, like the floor, were a jumbled mass of papers and newspapers. An old potbellied stove had small logs stacked beside it.

When Nancy opened the door, the premises were occupied only by Joe Hacker who sat at the desk hammering away at a typewriter in two-fingered but rapid style. He wore a heavy sweater and ski pants, evidently to compensate for the fact that his desk was at some distance from the stove.

He looked up as he felt the cold wind, pushed back his chair as he got to his feet. "Come in, Mrs. Gerard. Welcome to the Simonton *Weekly Gazette*. You may regard this as your home away from home. Everyone else seems to." He brushed papers off a chair onto the floor, drew the chair close to the stove. "Would you rather be too hot or too cold? That's the only choice I can offer you."

Something about his direct friendliness helped to dispel the cloud of doubt that had hung over her.

"This is just the way I've always pictured a great metropolitan newspaper office," she assured him.

He nodded. "The feverish activity, the endless shrilling of the telephone, the frenzied footwork to track down a story fifteen minutes ahead of the competition, the thrill of knowing tomorrow's news today. Well, anyhow, at least an hour ahead of the headlines."

When she had walked in she had looked as though she were facing a firing squad. Now she had relaxed and she was smiling at him. But this was no casual visit and she did not pretend that it was.

"Mrs. Hacker told me that you have something you want me to know, and that you don't want anyone else to guess I have come here. That's rather an odd request to make, isn't it?"

He leaned back in his swivel chair. "Perhaps. I play hunches. Instinct. Whatever people want to call it. My wife's all against this. She—we've made a pretty good thing of marriage. We've stayed in love and we like each other very much. Sometimes I think that's even more important. And Alice thinks there is no excuse for doing anything to cause trouble between a man and wife, particularly a bride and groom."

Nancy was silent. She watched him, her hands quiet on her lap.

"Well," he began heavily, "I'm still playing my hunch. Unless I am off my rocker, you are as straight as they come. Even personal considerations would not prevent you from doing what is right."

Even personal considerations. Nancy's heart felt cold but she still waited, unmoving but braced for a blow.

"You said you like Simonton." Nancy looked at him in bewilderment. "So do I, Mrs. Gerard. And Connecticut. And New England. And the United States. And the whole muddled world, if it comes to that. But just liking it, even loving it, is valueless. You remember Edith Cavell's words, just before the Germans shot her: 'Patriotism is not enough.' We have to work at it."

He looked at the still figure on the chair near the stove. "Agreed so far?"

"Of course."

"Well, Mrs. Gerard, the average citizen doesn't often face that gallant woman's situation. But we do have to cope with our problems when they arise, however small they may appear to be. Little problems neglected can grow into big ones."

He turned his chair so that he looked out on Simonton, a placid, sleepy New England village. Hibernating. Or was it?

"Something is wrong here," he said bluntly. "I thought there was nothing I didn't know about this place but someone is working against the government, trying to rally the malcontents under a single head, to build a party strong enough to take over the government."

Even personal considerations. Nancy's heart began to race. She held her hands quiet with an effort but she could not control her rapid breathing.

"The other day," Hacker said, "I was pawing through some of the junk on my desk looking for a news item I had mislaid, and I found three pieces of paper clipped together. The clip had caught on a folded page of a newspaper someone had been reading when he dropped in here. That stuff was dynamite. It consisted of directives for various student groups and political organizations that, as far as I know, have never had any open association."

"I don't understand."

"That stuff was left on my desk by mistake, which means it emanated from someone in this village."

"But this is horrible!" Nancy exclaimed. "Why don't you take it up with the government?"

"What have I got? Casual comments I've been hearing. Unrest I can't account for. Three sheets of paper which could be explained in a dozen ways. And the point is—I don't know who dropped them. I told you everyone in the village regards this as a home away from home; a place to gossip, to waste time, to pass on a little news item, to get some publicity when Johnny wins a school prize or a woman entertains her friends at bridge. Anyone in the whole damned place. And the danger of bringing in government men is that whoever is back of this thing will go underground."

"Haven't you any suspicions at all?"

"Oh, suspicions. Naturally."

Nancy took a long breath. "Why are you telling me this, Mr. Hacker?"

"The Gerards founded this village. They practically built it. More than anyone else, with the possible exception of the Wheelers, they have helped to maintain its essential quality." Hacker turned back from the window, saw the growing fear in her eyes. "To mastermind a thing like this takes three qualifications: brains, money, influence. No one has them to such a degree as Peter Gerard."

He brought his fist down on the table, startling her. "Mrs. Gerard, I've racked my brains; I've considered every posible alternative, but I keep coming back—"

"To Peter."

"I hope I'm wrong. That's why I—"

"Do you expect me to spy on my own husband, Mr. Hacker?"

"If I'm not wrong about you, I expect you to use your eyes, your ears, your brains, and the integrity that is

stamped all over you. I expect you to put the welfare of
your country above—"

"Even personal considerations."

"That's it."

She got up, squared her shoulders.

"What are you going to do, Mrs. Gerard?"

"I don't know," she told him.

II

I don't believe it. As Nancy walked home from the
newspaper office she kept repeating to herself, I don't
believe it. She did not doubt Joe Hacker's sincerity. He
believed that someone in Simonton was spearheading a
campaign against the government. There was no other
possible way the papers could have been lost in his office.
Someone had blundered. Blundered disastrously.

It occurred to her to wonder what would happen to Joe
Hacker if anyone should guess that the papers had been
left in his office. But Peter—surely Peter wouldn't—hurt
anyone.

Nancy's thoughts jolted her to a stop. She was assuming
that Peter was guilty. She made herself walk on again,
trying to think clearly. What did she know about this man
she had married? She remembered the long evening when
he had told her of his family, his heritage, the long brave
struggle of the Gerards to help build a new kind of
civilization.

No, she decided in relief, Peter isn't guilty. He can't be.
She went back to her original refrain, this time with a
light heart. *I don't believe it.*

She was still lighthearted while she dressed for dinner,
this time in ice blue. At the last moment she decided to
wear the pearl necklace. As usual, she found Peter in the
library, staring moodily into the fire, a pipe in his hand.
When he looked at her she thought in dismay that the
dress had been a mistake. He didn't like it.

"Very pretty pearls." He sounded like a stranger.

"They were my mother's, all I have that was hers."

"How's—Noah? I haven't seen him today."

"Neither have I," Nancy said guiltily. "I've been busy."

"That busy? You seem upset."

She flushed. She couldn't explain about her call on the editor. She said instead, "I am upset. I took Mrs. Hacker house-hunting and, Peter, do you know that the Maltby house is on the market? It should belong to the community. They can't sell it!"

"The Maltby house! Good Lord. It's one of the oldest in the country. We'll have—no, I don't like having Gerards throw their weight around. Look here, why don't you call Mrs. Wheeler? That's right up her alley. If the Historical Society can't swing the purchase, I'll step in, but I'd rather make it a community affair."

"I'll call her tomorrow," Nancy said.

The stiffness still remained in his manner. The strangeness. The restraint. It was a relief when dinner was announced.

Tonight, however, Peter was not as helpful as usual at keeping the conversation going before the servants. Every time Nancy looked up she found him watching her. She struggled as well as she could against the silence.

At length he asked, "Did Mrs. Hacker have any luck in finding a house she liked?"

"Now that's an odd thing!" Nancy told him about the farmhouse Mrs. Hacker had liked, about the wrong key and the new lock on a deserted house, about the cleared driveway and Max's insistence on entering the house first if the key worked. Max had been uneasy about the whole thing. He felt sure that the place was being used for some unauthorized purpose.

She had caught Peter's attention. As he got up from the table he said casually, "What did Hacker think about it?"

"I don't know."

When they were seated in the library, the coffee tray beside Nancy, Peter asked, "What did you and Hacker talk about?" and this time she looked into the hard eyes of a stranger.

"About you," she said at last. "He sent a message by Mrs. Hacker saying that he wanted to see me but he didn't want anyone to know."

"By anyone," Peter said evenly, "I assume you mean me."

"I mean you."

"It must be quite a secret if he expected you to keep it from your bridegroom. I suppose you agreed to this."

"I made no promise. He didn't ask for one. He just asked me to put integrity ahead of personal considerations. But I can't be that wrong about you, Peter. Perhaps I'm making a terrible mistake but I have to trust my own instinct."

She turned the wedding ring slowly around her finger. Then she gave him a complete account of her interview with the editor.

There was a long silence in the room before he asked, "What made you decide to tell me?"

"I discovered that I trust you completely. I know you are incapable of dishonor or disloyalty."

There was another pause. Then Peter said, "You haven't asked me any questions. Why?"

"Because all you asked of me was my trust."

He picked up her hand, kissed it lightly. "Thank you, Nancy. I have a telephone call to make and—"

She got up. "I'll go to bed. It's been a tiring day."

"Please wait. I just want to make sure someone keeps an eye on Hacker. Could be he is headed for trouble. Then I—"

"You knew about this!"

"I knew. That's why I am here. Wait until I have made my call and then I'll tell you all about it."

It was late when he finished the story that had begun in the dingy loft building on Fourteenth Street. "Now," he said, "you know as much about it as I do."

"Someone here in Simonton," Nancy said. "It's hard to believe."

"Someone I know," Peter said. "That's even harder. Just the same, I'll have to clear this with Hacker, and I'd like to put him on his guard."

"Do you think he could be in danger?"

"Well, let's put it his way. Someone around here is dangerous."

SIXTEEN

As NANCY pulled on ski pants and sweaters next morning she felt none of the usual exhilaration of indulging in winter sports, of the anticipation of feeling the wind on her face, the intoxication of skimming over the snow, or racing downhill on a bobsled.

"We'll try out our skis tomorrow," Peter had said the night before.

"Oh, that would be fun!" she had exclaimed in delight.

"Well, we really ought to be seen together." At his words her pleasure faded. Just a job to be done. "We'll try out that slope behind the house. Then we might go through the woods to that deserted house you and Mrs. Hacker found. Going that way won't seem as deliberate as though we headed straight for it."

All night the snow fell heavily and by morning a wind began to rise, bending tree tops, sending needles of snow into their faces.

"Are you going to be all right?" Peter asked. "I didn't bargain for anything like this."

"I'll be fine," Nancy assured him and led the way to the steep decline behind the grounds, where she stopped to put on her skis. Then with a shove she was off, soaring like a bird down the hill. At the bottom she turned to wave to him. "Nothing to it," she called. "A beginner's slope."

"If you say so," Peter replied dubiously, and found

himself moving much faster than he had expected. His skis seemed to have their own individual ideas as to where they wanted to go, and he completed the course by coasting on his face.

Nancy laughed when he got up, brushing off snow. "Hurt?"

"Just my pride."

"For a first attempt it wasn't bad."

"How did you guess it was a first attempt?" he said in mock indignation. "I warned you that I'd be a duffer."

"Well, you are certainly no threat to the Olympics," she agreed.

"We'll be knee-deep in snow," he warned her.

"But we can't wear skis through the woods."

"Then let's leave them here. We can pick them up tomorrow."

They walked side by side, sinking through the frozen snow, winding their way among the trees: pine and spruce, oak and maple, walnut and hemlock. Some of the branches were snowladen; from others dripped long, glistening spikes of ice.

"Warm enough?" Peter asked.

She nodded, her face glowing. "It's beautiful! Let people have their tropical nights; I'll settle for a snow-covered world on a winter day. It's just as beautiful and it's so much more challenging, more alive."

The woods appeared to be deserted but an occasional squirrel darted across the snow; a deer stood at the edge of a small clearing like a graven image and then, with a long leap, vanished behind trees. Low branches shook loads of snow on them as they passed.

They came out of the woods unexpectedly to find themselves on a side road. The wind was growing stronger, pelting them with ice particles, stinging their faces, their eyes. The snow was beginning to swirl in an ominous manner.

"We're going to have a blizzard," Nancy said, stopping for breath. "Thank heaven, we are out of the woods. It's so terribly easy to lose your sense of direction." She staggered as the wind struck her with sudden fury and

Peter caught her, put his arm around her, holding her against him.

"All right?"

"All right," she gasped, "but I'm glad we haven't much farther to go. That's the house, the one back of the picket fence. Heavens, the fence has been covered up, too!"

The gate stood open. Even with the snow swirling, it was possible to see traces of chains. A heavy truck had recently been here.

"I have a feeling we're too late," Peter said. "Just the same, I'd like to take a look."

"You can't get in without a key."

"There are windows." He moved closer, still holding her braced by his arm against the fury of the storm.

There was a sharp crack and he hurled Nancy to the ground, threw himself on top of her, using his body as a shield. Then there was no sound except for Nancy protesting, "Let me up, for heaven's sake. My face is so full of snow I can hardly breathe." He rolled to one side, still holding her down with his hand. "I suppose a branch broke under the weight of the snow." When Peter made no reply she asked sharply, "Did it hit you? Are you all right?"

"I'm all right. We're getting out of here, but keep down, Nancy. Don't stand up. Crawl."

She shook off his restraining hand, sat up, wiping her face clear of snow. "What's the matter with you?" Then she saw the blood on the snow.

"Peter! What happened? That branch—"

"That wasn't a branch. It was a rifle shot."

"A hunter?" She was bewildered. "But surely he could have heard our voices."

"There is someone in the house who doesn't want us to get any closer. Thank God, you didn't have the right key yesterday! Now let's get out of here."

"You are hurt."

"I'm all right. Start moving, Nancy. But crawl. Aim for those bushes. They aren't likely to risk a second shot if they think we are leaving. But—I can't take a chance with you."

He followed her, dragging himself along, using one el-

bow to help propel him as the other arm refused to obey
his commands. But always he kept between her and the
house.

"Now run!" he said.

With his arm around her shoulders, her arm around his
waist, they made as good time as was possible through the
heavy, swirling snow.

"At least," he grunted, "they can't see us here. We
should be safe now."

"I'll get you home."

"What I need first is a telephone."

After a look at his determined face she made no protest. "Then we'll try Mr. Hacker's office," she said.
"That's the nearest place. Anyhow, it's about time you
two pooled your stories, don't you think?" He staggered,
nearly making her lose her footing.

She looked at him anxiously. "Hold on. It's only about
a hundred yards more . . . only twenty yards . . . Just a
few steps." She flung open the door of the *Gazette*.

After one startled look, Hacker was across the room,
helping to ease Peter onto a chair.

"Got to telephone," Peter said thickly, and crumpled on
the floor.

When Nancy had called for Dr. Ferrell and an ambulance—she told Hacker the whole story.

"And as soon as we got there, Peter said we were too
late. There were chain marks on the snow. And someone
fired a rifle shot and hit Peter and finally we came here.
But you see what it means, don't you? Peter's not guilty!
He's on your side."

Hacker smiled at her exultant tone. "I'm as glad as you
are, Mrs. Gerard. But look here, all hell is breaking loose
in this village. We've never had violence before or any
serious crime. But last night someone broke in and tore
the office to pieces."

"Peter was afraid something might happen to you. Did
they get those papers?"

He grinned at her. "Believe it or not, I'm walking on
them right now."

"In your shoes?" Nancy began to laugh.

Dr. Ferrell's arrival, in a ramshackle car, was followed

almost immediately by an ambulance and two interns who lifted Peter onto a stretcher and carried him out.

After a brief examination Dr. Ferrell had said, "Just a deep flesh wound, thank God. He has lost a little blood. But you'll probably have him home in a day or two. You understand, don't you, Mrs. Gerard, that I'll have to report a bullet wound."

"Wait until you talk to Peter, Doctor. I understand that this must be reported but there is a man—Peter will tell you. Please do as I ask."

Several hours later, Peter, neatly bandaged, still very white, lay on a hospital bed, fuming.

"If you behave yourself you may be able to come home tomorrow," Nancy told him. "But if you carry on like this, they may keep you for days."

"But I have things to do. Urgent things."

"Tell me, and I'll do them for you."

"You're quite a girl, Nancy. All right, call the inn. Say that Mrs. Elwood would like to talk to Mr. Perkins. Tell him that his friend in the hospital is much better and would like to see him. Then go down to the waiting room. He'll get here as soon as possible. He looks—but you won't need to identify him. He'll know you."

"He will?"

"We saw you leaving Hacker's office. He said, 'That's a beauty!' "

"Oh."

"Tell him what happened, have him arrange things with the doctor, and then send him on to Joe Hacker. Also that empty farmhouse should be checked on at once. Even if they have moved everything out, whatever they had there, some prints may be found."

"Anything else?"

"That's all. Bless you, Nancy. Old Reliable. That's what I told Foster, the man you're to call as Mr. Perkins."

"Oh." Nancy added flatly, "That's very flattering."

Peter watched in surprise as she went out without saying good-by. She seemed rather flushed. His eyes closed and he slept.

I

There was nothing to do that evening except wait. Dr. Ferrell called to say Peter would be able to come home after another full day in bed. The FBI man, using the name of Mr. Perkins, telephoned to tell her that the house from which the bullet had been fired was empty. Someone was moving fast, faster than he—or they—had anticipated. He did not sound disappointed.

"Keep them on the run and they'll make mistakes," he told her cheerfully. He explained that he was telephoning from the newspaper office and that Hacker had been most helpful. He had turned over some very useful stuff.

"But you still don't know who left it there," Nancy pointed out.

"We're digging into the background of everyone who is even remotely possible. Just a matter of elimination. You've been careful, haven't you, not to mention Gerard's accident? Except to Max, of course."

Max was on guard duty in Peter's hospital room, armed with a revolver Foster had provided.

"I said Max had driven Peter to New York for a conference."

"Good."

That evening the library seemed less comfortable than usual. It felt empty. Nancy wandered restlessly up to her sitting room and telephoned Mrs. Wheeler about the Maltby house. As Peter had foreseen, Mrs. Wheeler was horrified.

"I'll call an emergency meeting of the Historical Society for day after tomorrow. We'll arrange to buy the place and restore it. My dear, how grateful I am to you. It would be a tragedy to have our oldest landmark disappear."

"How grateful Simonton should be to you, Mrs. Wheeler."

"Of course, you and Peter must come. The Gerards carry so much weight, and the destruction of our past is—well, it's an outrage."

There was still a lot of evening to get through. In her room Nancy looked down on the guesthouse. Noah was walking up and down, up and down. That was good. That was wonderful. That was why she had married Peter. She ought to be happy. She was happy, she told herself fiercely.

She cried herself to sleep.

II

After she had visited the hospital next morning, where she found Peter greatly improved, Nancy was again at loose ends. Max had driven her home and he went to his room to catch up on sleep. On her return, Murch told her that a large box had arrived, special delivery. Grateful for something to occupy her time—what was wrong with her, anyhow, that she was so restless?—she bundled up and took the package out to the guesthouse.

Noah was dressed and leaning back in his chair.

"Tired?" Nancy asked.

He smiled at her. "I've eaten so much breakfast I can't move."

"Here's the stuff you ordered, but why on earth—"

"Why did I want grease paints? Well, I'm going to fix up that idiot child, Helen Ferrell."

"But, Noah—grease paints!"

"Quiet, wench. I don't know anything about women's street make-up but I do know my way around with grease paints."

"But Helen can't go around all bedaubed—"

"I just want to teach her what to do. That girl's a submerged beauty and I'm going to shake some sense into her."

"The last time you were heavy-handed, she resigned," Nancy warned him.

"I'm a pitiful case," he told her cheerfully. "Helpless invalid. All alone."

"If she falls for that line she really is an idiot child," Nancy retorted.

As she slipped into her coat he said, "By the way, Peter told me the real story behind your marriage."

"I'm sorry."

"I insisted after I heard about that Barbee girl." Noah was watching her closely. "Peter says you'll be able to arrange an annulment without any difficulty."

"Oh, yes, I suppose so," Nancy agreed drearily. "But, Noah, you aren't to worry about me."

A smile twitched his lips. "I'm not worrying," he assured her. As she slammed the door she heard him chuckling. If that was all he cared for her happiness, her sacrifice—in her rage she nearly knocked Helen off her feet.

"Sorry, I didn't see you."

"I thought I'd see if—Neil—wanted anything."

"He told you he was Neil Carrington?"

"I guessed."

"Go ahead. He wants something, all right. But if he makes a play for sympathy I devoutly hope you'll laugh in his face."

Helen looked after her in surprise and then knocked on the door.

"Come in," Noah called cheerfully. He had cleared off a table and set out on it a box of grease paints.

"Where's Max?"

"He had to drive Peter to New York last night and just got back. He's in bed. Sit down. No, across the table."

"But why, Mr. Carrington?"

"Neil," he suggested. "Now then, tip your head up so I can see you. Mm. Yes. Well—" He dipped his fingers in a jar of cream and applied it lavishly to her face.

"What do you think you're doing?" she protested.

"Wiping off those cinders, Cinderella. Keep your eyes shut—and your mouth."

"I won't."

"Oh, yes, you will, Kitten."

After her first protests, Helen remained patiently quiescent while Neil worked at her face, her mouth, her eyes. Then he sat looking at her, head on one side.

"Something has to be done about your hair. You need a fluffy style with that narrow face. All right. All right. You can look at yourself."

He got his shaving mirror and set it before her. After a startled exclamation at the transformation, Helen said, "How did you do it?"

"I just emphasized the things you've tried to hide: your incredible eyes, that small straight nose, that sensitive mouth. Like it?"

She nodded shyly. "But I can't go around like this."

"Of course not. Before you clean off that grease, study the technique. Now straighten up. Walk as though you were proud of yourself. That's my Kitten." There was an insidiously caressing note in his voice which she had never heard before.

"I feel like something out of Pygmalion."

"And you know what happened to him, don't you, when the statue he created came alive? He went down for the count. Fell madly in love with his own creation." The laughter faded. Unconsciously he touched the scars on his face.

"Neil," she said eagerly, "why don't you—Physician, heal thyself. If it worked for me, it would work for you."

"It wouldn't."

"How do you know until you try?"

While she watched, he began to work with the grease paints. When he had finished, he made no comment at all, simply looked at her.

She drew a long breath. "The scars don't show! Neil, they don't show at all!"

Something of her own excitement affected him. "They would for a movie close-up, of course. But on the stage I just might get by with it." The excitement ebbed. "If it weren't for my memory, of course."

"Oh, that!" Helen dismissed the problem airily.

"Yes, that."

The violet eyes summed him up. "I always thought you were too good-looking to be true."

"And now?" he asked bitterly.

"I still do."

As he pulled himself out of his chair and started purposefully toward her, Helen laughed, caught up her coat, and ran for the door.

SEVENTEEN

PETER was still pale and his left arm was stiff but, by the time Max had driven him home from the hospital late the following afternoon and helped him dress for dinner, he was determined to accompany Nancy to the emergency meeting of the Historical Society at the Wheeler house. For some reason he seemed to be in excellent spirits.

When Nancy protested at his going out he shook his head at her warningly and she fell silent. Apparently he and the unassuming FBI man had made some plans but she was excluded from them. She smoldered with indignation. If it weren't for Noah, she thought, she would walk out. This very minute

While they had coffee in the library Peter told her that he had discovered her brother's identity.

"You understand now," she said, "why he didn't want people to know. Publicity like that could ruin his professional career. People would come to see him out of morbid curiosity rather than for his acting. But he is improving. Today he managed to cover the scars with grease paints so they barely show, even in daylight. As soon as he is able to leave—"

"Good lord," Peter said in alarm, "he mustn't get well too soon. I need him here. I need you both. It won't be long now."

It won't be long now. Then everything is fine, Nancy thought. Just fine. She looked at Peter's frowning face but he was staring at the fire, absorbed in his own thoughts. The clock on the mantel chimed the half hour.

"We'd better go," he said. "The Wheelers are sticklers about people being prompt."

"What do you want me to do?"

"Just tell them what you learned about the Maltby house and how you felt about it. But if the conversation becomes general, watch your step. I'm desperately afraid that the people we are looking for may be at the meeting tonight."

The Wheeler house was unexpectedly magnificent but on Nancy the effect was like being in a museum rather than a home. The great illuminated manuscript on the carved medieval lectern was as untouchable as an exhibit under glass. The chairs seemed too ancient to sit on. She was half surprised not to find velvet ropes shutting them off, or signs reading, "Do not touch."

Most of the members of the Historical Society were people whom she had already met at the open house. The Wheelers, gentle and formal, welcomed her. The Mortons were there with Mrs. Morton's protégé, Philip Miller. Dick Stowell came eagerly to welcome Nancy. The Hackers had been included, Nancy suspected, because the Wheelers hoped the weekly paper would feature the meeting and arouse public opinion in support of preserving historical landmarks.

When the meeting had been called to order, Nancy was asked to tell them what she had learned about the Maltby house. She did so warmly and with indignation. Then her part was over and she settled back to listen, her eyes moving from face to face. These were all nice people and yet, if Peter was right, one of them, perhaps even more, had become involved in a conspiracy that might be powerful enough to sway a national election.

A motion was offered to buy the old seventeenth-century structure and it was carried with only one dissenting vote. That came from Morton.

"It's a dismal old place," he complained. "No one could call it a beauty spot. I can't see why you want to keep it. You pay out good money for an eyesore. If that's what you want, why not be practical? Tear down the thing and put up a garage. That's a good corner and, as it is, we have to drive two miles to get gas or have repairs made. Does that make sense?"

When he was outvoted he gave up with a good-natured shrug. The business of the evening was quickly settled and the members of the committee formed groups, chatting as informally as was possible in the Wheeler environment.

At the first opportunity, Stowell buttonholed Peter. "I've got bad news for you," he said in a low voice.

Peter was startled. "What's that?"

Stowell told him about his lunch with Cynthia Barbee. "That girl is set for trouble. She claims you jilted her."

"There's no truth in that. We were engaged and she broke the engagement."

Stowell was worried. "She intends to get money out of you in one way or another."

Peter clapped him on the shoulder. "Cheer up! She can't get anywhere. Matter of fact, I was afraid you had fallen for her yourself."

"She's a pretty thing, but she has a cash register where her heart should be. Fear nothing, brother! Oh, by the way, young Miller tells me he has seen your paintings and they are great stuff. He dropped in at the inn when I had the illuminating lunch with Cynthia, too excited to wait."

"That's pleasant to hear." Peter turned away abruptly as Morton said, "Whenever I come to this house I always think we are still fighting the Revolution."

"In a sense we are," Peter replied. "The struggle for freedom never ends. We correct one abuse and another emerges. There's no time when a man can afford to stand aside or refuse to stand up and be counted."

A maid caught Peter's attention. "Telephone call for you, sir."

In Wheeler's study Peter picked up the handset. "Gerard speaking."

"This is—" The words were so muffled that Peter could not make them out.

"Noah." The voice was clearer now but still low. "I thought you'd be interested to know that your prowler is back."

Peter talked fast.

I

Max, who had still not caught up on his sleep, was relieved when Noah said, "I'll read for a while before I go to bed. I won't need a thing."

When the chauffeur had gone upstairs to his room, Noah put down his book, noticing that his hand was not as startlingly thin as it had been. He was beginning to put on weight. Slowly, of course, but still an improvement. The exercises provided by Dr. Ferrell had already made it possible for him to get around without too much difficulty. Tomorrow, he would try walking out of doors, unless there was more snow.

But the staggering thing was that, by a careful use of grease paints, he would be able to cover the scars on his face until they eventually faded, as he had been assured they would. It was hard to make so quick an adjustment from the time when he had regarded himself as a monster, when the blond girl had run from him.

He switched out the lights and leaned back in his chair, musing. The blond girl was poison and she would do her best to spoil things for Nancy and Peter. So far as his brother-in-law was concerned, Noah thought he could take care of himself, but he wasn't so sure about Nancy.

How like her it had been to make that impulsive marriage in order to look after him! He wondered if she knew that she had fallen in love with her husband. One thing was sure: Peter didn't know it. How far would he be justified in interfering? True, Peter had betrayed some jealousy over Nancy's interest in the man Neil Carrington. After considering the matter, Noah decided there was nothing he could do. If Peter didn't want Nancy, if he were to maintain their marriage out of a sense of obligation—no, never.

Tomorrow, he would read to Helen. Which of his roles had she liked best? Hotspur. If only his memory could be relied on, he would be ready to go back to the theater in another three months. He wondered uneasily whether Helen would like theatrical life, an upside-down sort of life.

Then it occurred to him that he was taking a lot for granted. It was one thing for a girl to respond to a sick man's needs, to help him pass some otherwise empty hours. But when he didn't need her any more, she might not be interested.

He thought of the dark-fringed violet eyes. He would always need her. He would marry her if he had to carry her off screaming, like Petruchio. And he had better hurry. Now that she had come out of her shell, he would have a lot of competition. At least, she would never be Cinderella again.

The trouble was, Noah reflected, that while he would always need Helen, she wouldn't need him any more. He had given her back to herself. Why should she care about a man so much older than she was when she could have any number of younger ones at her feet?

There was a flicker of light around the corner of the big house. Someone was moving cautiously, holding a flashlight. The beam touched the path, moved on to the darkened window, to the door of the guesthouse.

Noah groped for the telephone, dialed the operator, asked for the Wheeler house. When he had talked to Peter, he moved toward the stairs.

"Max!" It was only a whisper. "Max!" He spoke again, keeping his voice as low as possible.

There was a grunt, the bedsprings in the room above creaked.

"Quiet! We've got our prowler back. I called Gerard. He said to provide a welcoming committee and then hold him."

Max started down noiselessly. "Where are you?" he whispered.

"At the table."

"Get down out of sight."

The handle of the door was turned, turned again. Then there was a click as the lock was forced. The door opened, inch by cautious inch, so silently that the two men who waited tensely were aware of it only because of the icy draft that swirled around their feet.

In the darkness of the night it was impossible to see who stood in the doorway, who moved forward gropingly, and then eased the door shut behind him. Max and Noah were motionless. The flashlight beam crept along the floor, touched Noah's open but empty bed, the table and chairs, the staircase. Rested on Max.

Everything seemed to happen at once. There was a startled gasp from the intruder, Noah pushed himself up from the floor where he had been crouching, Max leaped down the last few steps toward the door, a shot rang out, and the door was flung open.

Lights were switched on and Peter plunged into the room followed by Foster. Noah blinked in the light. Max lay on the floor, blood seeping from a shoulder wound, and the ferret-faced man wheeled, gun in hand.

"Drop it," Foster said, his gun steady.

An automatic fell from the intruder's hand and he submitted sullenly while Foster handcuffed him. Peter was kneeling beside Max. The latter looked up at him, managed a grin.

"Get Dr. Ferrell," Peter told Noah who reached for the telephone.

"I'm okay. Felt like a hammer blow. Gosh," Max said in surprise, seeing the blood on his shoulder, "he shot me."

"It's just a flesh wound, so far as I can tell." Peter brought a towel to stanch the blood, and then looked at the prowler. "And who is this?"

"This," Foster said, "is Miss Barbee's brother, *alias* William Barnes, *alias* Wilton Brooks, *alias* Willis Benton, *alias* Mr. Nemeau. Mr. Nobody. The prints check."

Peter ran his fingers through his hair. "I can't figure this, Foster. What has this guy—whatever his name is— got to do with—"

Foster made a warning gesture and Peter stopped abruptly.

"This," the FBI man said, "seems to be a separate operation. What were you looking for?" When the man of many names made no reply he repeated, "What were you looking for in the guesthouse? We've got you dead to rights, Mr. Nobody. Talk."

"Let's see your credentials."

Foster held out his open wallet and Mr. Nobody's eyes

popped. "Oh, my God! The Feds. I haven't done anything to bring you boys down on my head."

"What were you looking for? I can keep this up longer than you can, Mr. Nobody, and when I get tired I can call in a lot of others."

"Okay. Okay. Only you got to see this my way."

"Have I indeed?" Foster said softly.

"My sister got a lousy break. This guy jilted her. She has a right to something, hasn't she? He's a rich guy."

"So you think he's a sucker. What were you looking for?"

"Cynthia says there's no safe in the house. She looked everywhere."

"Oh." Peter was enlightened. "You were after the diamond necklace and thought the safe might be out here." He began to laugh. "You know, the funny thing is that I bought that necklace for Cynthia. I had it in my pocket the afternoon she turned me down and said I wasn't her type."

The men watched in open amusement the change of expression on Mr. Nemeau's face. "God!" he muttered at last. "When Cynthia knows this she'll blow her top!"

Peter opened the door to admit Dr. Ferrell, who bent over to examine his patient. When he stood up at last he said, "What are you trying to do, Gerard? Turn Simonton into a shooting gallery? Two gunshot wounds in three days!"

"I wasn't doing the shooting. Last time, if you remember, I was on the receiving end."

The doctor turned to Foster. "Are you taking the responsibility again?" He glared at Mr. Nemeau. "We can do without people like that in this town."

"You won't have him long," Foster assured the doctor. "He's moving on tonight."

"Look here," Mr. Nemeau whined, "I know my rights. I want a lawyer."

"You'll need him. Out!" At the door Foster turned, one wrist shackled to his prisoner. "I'd appreciate a little peace and quiet for the rest of the night."

Peter laughed. "We all would. Doctor, shall I call an ambulance?"

"I can fix him up here if you will help me get him to bed."

"Max can have mine," Noah suggested, "and I'll take his. Save him the stairs."

"Where's my daughter? Helen is good at fetching and carrying. I could use her."

"You aren't going to," Noah assured him.

II

Nancy put down her pen on the inlaid desk in the morning room which still bore the scar where Peter had smashed his pipe.

"What happened last night?" she asked as he came into the room. "Helen says she heard a shot, and Murch says you didn't go to bed at all. And you just out of the hospital."

He began to laugh. "Actually, it was rather funny." He described the attempt of Cynthia's brother to find the diamond necklace and how he had shot Max.

Baffled, Nancy shook her head. "I'll never understand men. What's so funny about that? And I'll bet Max isn't laughing his head off."

"It was only a flesh wound. Painful but not serious."

"Then Max seems to be all right?"

"Noah is looking after him today. He says that turn and turn about is fair play."

"But I still don't see what was so funny."

"The joke is that Cynthia could be driven to trying to steal a necklace I bought for her in the first place." Peter leaned back in his chair and yawned widely. "Sorry."

"You are asleep on your feet."

He got up, yawned again. "I'm going to bed now and catch up. Tonight, I'll be busy."

"What are you up to?" she asked suspiciously.

He shook his head, smiling.

"You aren't going to do anything—dangerous, are you?" There was a quaver in her voice.

He answered too promptly. "Of course not. Just a little prowling around."

"Can't I help?"

He patted her shoulder. "Old Reliable. Where's Helen?"

"Getting a permanent wave. Noah's orders. He says she is a submerged beauty."

His eyebrows went up in surprise. "What goes on there?"

"I think they are falling in love."

"Well—" This time the yawn nearly dislocated his jaw.

Nancy laughed. "You get some sleep. I'll see Noah and keep an eye on Max."

She found both men dressed and in cheerful spirits. Men, she pointed out to them, were certainly odd.

"Nothing like a little gun battle to shake a man out of the doldrums," Noah assured her.

"I'll bet Max doesn't feel that way."

"I still feel surprised. Like a heavy blow. Not at all what you'd expect."

"I hope I never find out," Nancy said fervently.

When Helen appeared, rather self-conscious about her first permanent wave, her face carefully but discreetly made up, Nancy looked at her in amazement. Noah had been right. The girl was lovely and she had acquired a new assurance.

Back at the house Nancy found herself pacing restlessly. Things were happening and she didn't know what they were. It was late in the afternoon when Foster telephoned. "Mr. Perkins," a maid told Nancy.

At his request, she agreed to meet him at the edge of the village. When she got there he was waiting. Once more he marveled at Gerard's good luck. He had seen her close up for the first time when he met her in the lobby of the hospital. The girl was not only a beauty; her direct gaze had intelligence behind it, her mouth had character behind it, her handshake had warmth behind it. But all this seemed to be wasted on Gerard. His had been a matter-of-fact faith in her reliability, which was not the usual response of a man to a beautiful woman who also happened to be his wife.

"I understand you and Peter had some excitement last night," she said.

He nodded. "That's why I am here. I need your help, Mrs. Gerard."

"Of course."

He smiled. "No hesitation?"

"You are Uncle Sam in person. What can I do for you?"

"Gerard has put you in the picture, I understand."

"He wasn't betraying a trust." She spoke defensively. "I'd already learned about the situation from Mr. Hacker."

"I know, and I must say the Hackers are being most cooperative. The thing is, Gerard and I are going to be busy tonight. The chauffeur isn't up to much with that bandaged shoulder. Your brother is an invalid. It's not wise to take the servants into our confidence because, though they are trustworthy, some of them are local people and things get around. We could bring in extra men, of course, but the village is so small they'd be conspicuous and we don't want to alarm anyone. Do you know how to use a revolver?"

"Heavens, no!"

"Then," Foster said, "we are going out in the woods. We are going to have some target practice before the light fails."

EIGHTEEN

THAT NIGHT the Hackers gave a small dinner party at the inn for the Mortons, Philip Miller, and Cynthia Barbee. The young painter accepted eagerly when he learned that the pretty blonde was to be a guest.

The ferret-faced Mr. Nemeau had departed from the inn as unexpectedly as he had arrived. By lunchtime Cynthia was in a state of nerves. She did not know what had happened. She had not been surprised when her brother failed to appear for breakfast. As he had told her, after nearly a year in prison, from now on, for the rest of his life, he'd sleep as late as he chose. But by lunchtime she was uneasy.

There were two possibilities, neither of which pleased her. Either her brother had succeeded in finding the diamond necklace and had decided to keep the proceeds for himself, or he had failed to find it and had been caught. But in that case, what had happened to him? She had no illusions about her brother. If he believed he could get away with the necklace without sharing, he would not hesitate. But if he were caught, he would be only too eager to blame her for the robbery, relying on her former influence over Peter Gerard or the latter's dislike for scandal.

By mid-afternoon Cynthia was pacing the floor. By late afternoon she was standing at the window, awaiting the arrival of the police.

She accepted Mrs. Hacker's invitation to dinner with

surprise but some relief. Anything was better than this endless waiting. She prepared for dinner with her usual care, slipped over her head a brilliant red dress and arranged her soft blond curls. Seeing her reflection in the mirror, she blew a kiss to the pretty girl. "You'll get by," she told herself confidently and she went downstairs.

Mrs. Hacker met her with unexpected cordiality. "How nice of you to join us, Miss Barbee. I do think a dinner party is more successful if there is a pretty girl to look at."

"How sweet of you," Cynthia gushed, and turned to Morton, who was beaming at her. She had always found women a waste of time.

Joe Hacker was talking to Mrs. Morton who, as usual, was a shade overdressed, but who seemed genuinely pleased to be invited.

"Now this," she declared, "is really neighborly. People are rather slow about getting acquainted here, aren't they?" There was a wistful sound in her voice. "And to ask Philip, too! He was so pleased. Where—oh, he's talking to that pretty blonde."

"I understand you've done a great deal for that young man," the editor said.

"Not so much. We pay his living expenses, of course, but he lives on so little that I don't feel we should receive much credit."

"I hadn't realized before that you were an art patron."

"I'm not really."

"I take it you like abstract paintings."

"Well," she said vaguely, "I know what I like. I can't say I see much in all those splashes of color Philip throws on everything. I mean they aren't pretty, are they? And one I saw—just a lot of thick black lines up and down. But I suppose you have to keep up with new things." She seemed dubious about this.

"At least, he is fortunate to have an old friend to give him a helping hand."

"Goodness, Philip isn't an old friend. My husband met him somewhere just before we moved up here. It was his idea, really." Mrs. Morton flushed. "Simonton, say what you will, is rather exclusive. My husband felt that if I helped out a young artist it would give me more prestige."

"A sound idea," Hacker agreed dryly.

"And it isn't as though Philip costs much. Have you seen that place of his? Just a shack, really. On Pleasant Street. Such a queer name for the only really poor street in the village."

I

Pleasant Street was only a block long, with half a dozen houses on either side of the road, their curtains drawn against the cold night. In most of the houses lights burned in the kitchen, which served as dining room as well. Only one house was dark, a small corner building that once had served as a one-room schoolhouse and had been converted, more or less, by the addition of plumbing, electricity, and a space heater, into living quarters.

The door was brightly illuminated by a corner streetlight.

"Better leave this to me," Foster said. While Peter shielded a light, the FBI man slid back the lock. When they were inside and had made sure the curtains were drawn, Foster turned on the light and laughed.

"Handy little gadget," he said, showing a piece of thin celluloid. "This is what Mr. Nobody used last night."

"Has anyone got in touch with Cynthia yet about his arrest?"

Foster shook his head. "Mrs. Hacker watched the telephone at the inn all day and says the girl hasn't had any calls or made any; also she has been acting like a cat on hot bricks."

"Mrs. Hacker didn't mind inviting her to dinner?"

Foster chuckled. "I think she is enjoying all this mystery right up to the hilt, and Hacker is a born crusader. He intends to see that Simonton is cleaned up if he has to do it singlehanded."

"Good man."

Foster looked around the cluttered room. At one end, a sink was piled with dirty dishes. On a two-burner gas stove canned beans had grown cold in a kettle. Ashtrays overflowed with cigarette butts. There was a worn leather chair with a reading lamp. But most conspicuous were the paintings that covered the walls.

"Tell me," Foster said, after he had recuperated from the first impact, "what is this stuff supposed to mean?"

Peter laughed. "It's not supposed to mean anything. That's just the painter expressing himself."

"But can the man really paint?"

"He can certainly draw. But for some reason he has splashed color on the canvases with all the finesse of a house painter."

"Well, let's get to work. There's nothing to hold those people at the inn after ten o'clock though Hacker said he'd do his best. We have a lot to do."

"Where do we start?"

"Anywhere, so long as we don't duplicate efforts or miss anything." Foster moved briskly toward the kitchenette and began a slow, painstaking search.

Peter pinched his lower lip between his fingers, frowning. For a man who couldn't exhibit stuff like this anywhere except at a sidewalk display or a community charity, Philip Miller had done a lot of paintings. Of course, there was no reason why he should not be a bad painter if he could afford it, and with the Mortons' help, he seemed able to afford it. What had alerted Foster was the speed with which he had come to look at Peter's work. Someone had wanted to know how much truth there was in Peter's excuse for staying in Simonton.

While Foster was diligently investigating the floor for loose boards, Peter turned to the canvases. Never in his life had he seen paint laid on so thickly, so—he leaned closer, peered at the heavy red splotches across a canvas. He picked up a palette knife, used it cautiously.

"Foster!"

The FBI man turned around. "Look, Gerard, we have no time to waste on an art show; we have work to do."

"Come here." Carefully Peter scraped off paint, lifted a piece of transparent tape, and revealed a hundred-dollar bill.

"Well, I'll be—" Foster drew it out. There were four more under it—and eight similar packets taped neatly above and below it on the same canvas.

One by one, Peter scraped away the thickest paint on the other canvases, in each case revealing several thousand dollars in hundred-dollar bills. While he worked, Foster jotted down numbers and then replaced the money under the tape.

"Are you going to leave it here?" Peter protested. "We've found $20,000 and it looks like there may be much more."

"Can you cover up again?"

"I'll do my best." Rapidly Peter mixed paints and sloshed them over the tape. Technique was of no importance as long as he got the color right.

"I doubt if he'll know the difference," Foster said. "Hey, don't light your pipe in here. The smell of tobacco will be a dead giveaway. Okay, let's get out of here. It's after nine-thirty and time is running out on us."

They let themselves quietly out of the house and did not speak until they had reached the avenue.

"How do you see it?" Peter asked.

"Miller is the boy who is making the contacts. The money must be for the people whose support he is buying. They don't dare use checks. They won't want to take the risk of sending the money by mail in case the wrong person opens the letters. But a painting—"

"What I want to know," Peter began, "is—"

"Whose cash?"

"Yes."

"What leaps to the eye, of course, is friend Morton whose wife doesn't sound like an art patron."

"Just the same—" Peter sounded dissatisfied.

"What are you trying to do? Make things difficult?"

"No. I think you are right about Miller being the contact man. Morton sounds most likely as the guy who is doing the financing, and he is right psychologically, too. He'd like power and he has no respect for democratic processes. But—"

"Well?"

"Well, Foster, he is not essentially a man of imagination. He's more like one of those impressive puppets set up by the real dictators. He just doesn't have the brains."

"At any rate, he's in this thing right up to his neck." Foster stopped. "This is his place, isn't it?"

"Yes, but we'll have to be careful. The Mortons have four servants."

"A house with four servants isn't apt to have many secrets. What interests me is that three-car garage with the big workshop beside it."

"After all, they have three cars, and Morton does a lot of puttering around out there. Hobby of his."

"Well, we can't stand here all night."

The Morton place was a big white Colonial of perhaps twenty rooms, set back on spacious grounds. It was not only well-lighted within, but outside lights had been left burning for the absent owners. The driveway had been plowed and sanded.

The two men felt uncomfortably conspicuous as they went down the driveway. Foster pointed out in a whisper that there were no pedestrians on the avenue to see them and it was unlikely the servants would be looking out on the street where nothing moved, but they were relieved to get around the side of the house and out of range of the lights.

One garage door stood open. The other two were closed. Softly the two men stole toward the workshop. Then the silence was shattered by the baying of a huge dog. The two men retreated as silently as they had come.

NINETEEN

PETER had gone out before dinner, slipping a note under the door of Nancy's sitting room.

"I've explained to Murch that I have another conference. There's nothing to worry about. Peter."

Nothing to worry about. He had gone without seeing her, so as to escape her inevitable questions. After all, he had a right to do that. His private affairs did not concern her.

The house seemed too big and too empty. Too lonely. She asked for a tray in her sitting room. No point in dressing for dinner tonight. She had put on soft green velvet lounging pajamas and matching slippers with absurd high heels.

When Murch brought the tray she tried to eat. *Nothing to worry about*. Beside her, thrust down in the chair where the butler could not see it, her fingers touched the revolver the government agent had left with her.

Somewhere, out in the night, Peter and Foster were, as Peter had put it, prowling around. About all she was sure of was that they had not gone to the farmhouse. Foster had told her, during her practice session at target shooting, that the house was empty, that it had been wiped clean of prints. The man with the rifle had gone away without leaving a trace. But he must be somewhere near at hand. He had ransacked Hacker's office looking for those missing papers. He would be frantic, wondering where and how he could have mislaid them. He wouldn't give up the search because he couldn't afford to. That, of course, was why Foster had given Nancy the gun and made sure she knew how to use it.

When her tray, barely touched, had been removed, she turned on her small radio, found Leontyne Price singing *Aida*. How tragic love was in opera, but how beautiful. The effortless voice rang out and then the program was over.

"More cold in store for the New England states," the announcer said briskly.

Nothing to worry about. It doesn't concern me, Nancy told herself firmly. Whatever Peter is doing tonight, whatever danger he may be in, it doesn't concern me. I'm not really his wife. Remember that he said he would never think of another woman as his wife. I'm just Old Reliable.

A finger touched cold metal and she shivered. I'm not brave at all, she thought. I'm frightened. Frightened for Peter. If anything happened to him—and suddenly, from the wave of desolation that swept over her, she knew the truth. She loved Peter.

She felt as though a bandage had been removed from her eyes and she could see clearly for the first time. This was why she had been so anxious for his approval, so hurt when he had shut her out of his confidence, so upset when Noah had reminded her that Peter would arrange for the annulment. Noah had guessed about her. She felt a wave of embarrassment and then lifted her head proudly. She wasn't ashamed of loving Peter. She gloried in it. But—but Peter hadn't asked for her love. He didn't want it. He had been alarmed about Noah recuperating too soon simply because he needed them both. *It won't be long now,* he had assured her.

She tried to imagine what her life would be like when she left this house, this dear room, for the last time. Noah would soon be well. Helen had done more for him than he had for her, challenged him, made him forget his troubles, interested him in someone else. Perhaps they would marry. It would, she thought, be a good marriage. Noah would give Helen the confidence she lacked; she would help to modify and soften the actor's egotism.

A good marriage like the one the Hackers had built between them. Still in love and, he had said, "We like each other." Something solid and enduring beyond the radiance of passionate love. A key to many doors.

Nancy stared unseeingly at the carpet under her frivolous slippers. But Peter held the only key that mattered, the key to his own heart. That's one lock no one can force, she thought, and found herself considering Cynthia who had known how to open that lock. Peter's face and voice the day he had met her in the Museum were clear before Nancy's eyes. Cynthia knew all a woman's tricks, she had all the guile.

No! Nancy was ashamed. She wouldn't want Peter on those terms. If everything could not be honest between them, nothing would have value.

She sat up. Someone was coming quietly up the stairs. Her heart leaped. Peter was home, he was safe. She was not aware of how anxious she had been until the wave of relief swept over her.

Peter's door opened and closed quietly, so she knew that he did not intend to talk to her tonight. A little desolately, she got up to go to bed. For a moment she stood at her bedroom window. There were lights on the snow. Peter's studio had no shades. But he didn't work by artificial light, she remembered, and, after two strenuous days, he surely would not be painting at all.

Nancy went swiftly to the door, turned back to pick up the revolver. For a moment she looked at the telephone but there was no point in disturbing either Noah or Max. Neither of them was in condition to put up a fight. She took a long steadying breath and, holding the revolver in her right hand, she crossed the hall and eased open Peter's door.

The bedroom was dark but the studio beyond was lighted. Someone was moving around. There were only scatter rugs on the floor of the bedroom, she remembered, and she stepped out of her slippers so she could move without any betraying tap of high heels. She wasn't frightened now; she was angry. While Peter was seeking this man, he was searching Peter's studio. And this must be the man with the rifle, the man who had shot Peter.

The man, a furry cap over his head, stocking tied over his face, was pushing canvases around impatiently. Then his eyes caught a glint of green velvet, went up to her face, saw the hand holding the revolver.

He came at her in a rush, lunging for the gun, and Nancy pulled the trigger. Why it really works, she thought in surprise, and then something slammed against her head.

I

Dr. Ferrell looked down at Nancy. "I thought the Gerards were turning Simonton into a shooting gallery, but it is becoming more like a battlefield."

Helen stood beside the bed, looking white and shocked. In the corridor outside, the agitated butler was telling the servants to go back to bed.

"Was I shot?" Nancy asked, bewildered.

"Knocked out, but you had a gun in your hand. Someone fired it."

"I did. Has he got away?"

"He got away but I think you nicked him. There were blood spots across Mr. Gerard's room and down the stairs." The doctor added, "I suppose I report this to that—" He caught Nancy's warning gesture.

"Yes, please. Some day we'll explain the whole thing to you."

"Murch wanted to get the state police but I told him to hold off until Mr. Gerard returns home to give the orders. Do you know where your husband is?"

Nancy shook her head and then wished she hadn't.

"It will hurt for a while," the doctor said, observing her wince of pain. "Quite a lump you've got. But no more than a headache."

"Who found me?"

"Murch heard a shot, then someone tore down the stairs and out the front door. He found you unconscious in Mr. Gerard's bedroom, roused the house, and called me. If he weren't such a sound sleeper, none of this would have happened."

"What do you mean?"

"Someone seems to have ransacked the library, and no one heard it. Now, Mrs. Gerard—"

"Must you bother her now?" Helen protested, and for the first time her father noticed the transformation in the girl.

"Don't interrupt," he said curtly. "Mrs. Gerard—"

"I saw the lights from Peter's studio reflected on the snow and I knew, after what he'd been through, he wouldn't be working in there. So I went to see who it was."

"Carrying a revolver. Very sensible."

"No wonder Helen left home," Nancy snapped at him. "The man you met after Peter was shot gave me this gun this afternoon and taught me how to use it. When I saw the masked man coming at me I shot him. That's all I remember."

"I don't know what's going on here but I won't permit Helen to stay in the house any longer. People exchanging shots like a Grade B Western movie. And why your husband walked off, leaving you to face a burglar—"

Downstairs both Murch and Mrs. Henning were trying to speak at the same time. Then Peter cut in sharply, "Shot!" He ran up the stairs and down the corridor, flung open the sitting room door. "How bad is it?" he demanded.

Dr. Ferrell went to join him. "You'll have to check the library yourself. Murch doesn't know what might have been taken."

"I mean my wife."

Nancy's heart lurched. *My wife.* Then she remembered Peter's scathing words on their wedding night, "If you think for a moment I'll forget what your position here really is, you're a very stupid girl."

"She has a headache," Ferrell said dryly. "I didn't call the state police because your government friend seems to be taking all responsibility. But some other doctor will."

"Why?"

"Because," and the doctor chuckled, "your wife shot the burglar." He came back into the bedroom to get his bag. "It would be nice if you could postpone any more bloodshed until morning. Even a country doctor has to sleep now and then."

"You know," Nancy said, "I think when people know how good you are, you'll have more than a country practice here."

Then Peter was in the room. The evening must have been rugged for him, too. He was colorless. He pulled a chair beside her bed, reached for her hand.

"Can you tell me about it now or would you rather not?"

"Of course I can tell you." Her head moved restlessly.

"Another pillow?" He lifted her, reached for a pillow, holding her gently against his shoulder. For a moment she rested there. He bent over, his cheek brushing her hair, then his lips touched her forehead. "Good girl," he said lightly, and settled her on the pillows.

Odd that she had thought him colorless. There was a lot of color in his face now. He pushed his chair away from the bed.

"What happened?"

When she had finished he said quietly. "I could kill Foster for that! Running you into danger." He sounded as though he were angry with her. "My God, Nancy, didn't you have sense enough not to go barging in on a masked man, brandishing a gun? You were asking for trouble."

"Well, I had an idea——"

He groaned.

"Instead of bullying me," she said with some spirit, "you'd better see how much damage was done in the library."

"I couldn't care less about the library. And I'm getting to the point where I'm afraid to leave you alone for a single minute. No telling what trouble one of your impulses is going to lead to."

The unexpected anger in his voice brought an angry response from her. "It couldn't be worse than the trouble I landed in when I married you."

"Sorry." His face was without expression. "Sleep well, Nancy." He went out to the pretty sitting room and said in surprise, "I didn't know you were still here, Helen."

"I'll be here all night. I told my father so. There's nothing to worry about, Mr. Gerard."

Nothing to worry about. And that, Nancy thought, is where I came in. She pushed away the extra pillow, settled her throbbing head as comfortably as she could, and slid down the healing darkness of sleep.

II

While Helen caught up on sleep the next morning— that seemed to be the pattern of the topsy-turvy world into which she had been catapulted—Nancy dressed in blue wool and fastened a blue scarf over her hair to conceal the swelling on her head. There had been a brutal strength about her masked attacker the night before that had appalled her.

The maid who brought her breakfast tray was excited and wildly curious. "But we've never had burglars here before, madam! And nearly killing you, too."

Nancy smiled. "I think I came nearer to killing him."

"A gun! We were all saying you are the bravest thing." The girl flushed.

"Not really. I was scared to death."

"And Mr. Gerard away at the time."

With any encouragement the girl would go on and on. That much drama had never entered her life before. To sidetrack her Nancy asked, "Where is Mr. Gerard?"

"In the library, madam." The maid flung up her hands. "It's a sight."

"Tell him, please, that I'll be down in a few minutes."

Nancy found herself walking as softly as she could because her head pounded with every step. When she entered the library, Joe Hacker was with Peter. For a moment she stood horrified by the mess.

"I don't understand why none of us heard it!" she exclaimed.

"This required speed, not noise," Peter said. "How is your head?"

"I hope, if I'm careful, it will stay on."

"Well, see that you are careful." Peter still sounded

angry. He pulled out a chair for her. "Hacker has a tale to unfold. Go ahead, man!"

The editor looked at Nancy. "I must say for a girl who got banged on the head you seem surprisingly well."

"Go ahead," Peter said impatiently. "I may have to leave at any minute."

Hacker smiled at Nancy. "That husband of yours is a born tyrant. Personally, I suspect he was the one who hit you. All right, man, I'll talk. Hold your horses."

He described the dinner party at the inn the night before. Cynthia, he said, had been watched unobtrusively all day by his wife. No one had got in touch with her.

"What did you learn from the party?" Peter asked.

"Not much, considering we had them on our hands for over three hours, but a few points of interest. Mrs. Morton is no art patron. She doesn't know a Rembrandt from a Picasso and she cares less. This sponsorship of Philip Miller, whom, by the way, she never heard of until just before they moved to Simonton, was her husband's idea. He told her it would help them enter Simonton society."

"Well?"

"There was nothing concrete. Miller made a big play for the blonde but, though she would flirt with a barracuda if nothing better offered, she wasn't really interested. No smell of money about Miller."

You might be surprised, Peter thought, remembering the money he and Foster had found in the painter's studio.

"But Morton really let himself go. He doesn't think the average person is capable of self-government or deserving of education. He'd like to see our college education limited to the people who are natural leaders, people like himself, I assumed. He would like to see books censored. He doesn't like a free press or free speech. They just confuse people who would rather be told what to think."

"It must," Peter said mildly, "have been a delightful evening."

"Well," Hacker replied philosophically, "once as a boy I had to clean out a pigpen. No life can be a bed of roses."

The telephone rang and Peter reached for it. "Yes," he said. "Yes, I'm leaving now."

He turned to say, "Sorry, this is important. Thank you more than I can say, Hacker."

"All I want to know is—was it helpful?"

"It's always helpful to clean out pigpens." Peter turned to Nancy. "You behave yourself. No impulses. Don't go anywhere. Don't get any ideas." Seeing Hacker's speculative glance he bent and kissed her slowly, lingeringly on the mouth.

TWENTY

AFTER the gray station wagon had turned onto Route Seven and had begun to follow the winding course of the icebound Housatonic River, Foster relaxed. At first Peter had been somewhat dubious about the adequacy of the shabby car but when the FBI man stepped on the gas to pass a truck he gave an exclamation of surprise.

"This heap is a lot better under the hood than it looks," Foster said cheerfully. "Our boys do these things rather well."

"All kinds of tricks," Peter said, "like putting a gun in my wife's hand. I suppose you know she was knocked out last night."

Foster gave a stifled exclamation and Peter told him of the masked man who had torn the library apart and had started on the studio when Nancy interrupted him.

"Looking for the papers, of course. Well, we've got them safe."

"But he struck Nancy! Look here, Foster—"

"She knew exactly what she was up against. We use the weapons we have, Gerard. Sometimes we don't like them but we have no choice."

"As of now," Peter said, "you have no choice. Don't try to involve my wife in anything more. Is that clear?"

Something in his cold anger made Foster say amiably, "Clear as daylight. Anyhow, we are closing in. The station wagon ahead is loaded with—"

"Canvases, of course. Is Miller on the run?"

"I doubt it. He is probably making one of his regular deliveries."

"How do you suppose he gets rid of the stuff?"

"You're the painter. How would you go about it?" The government agent thought it was better to get Gerard's mind off his smoldering anger. A lot worse things happened to people than bumps on the head. A lot worse might happen if this thing weren't stopped.

To his relief, Peter gave the problem his consideration. "I think I'd subsidize a crooked art dealer—and, unfortunately, the woods are full of them. He could ship out the canvases, one at a time, without arousing suspicion."

As they approached New York and traffic grew heavier, it was easier to avoid notice but harder to keep the station wagon in sight. At each exit the men watched sharply. To their surprise the car went down the Henry Hudson Parkway, past the lyrical span of the George Washington Bridge, past the squat tomb of General Grant, down and down.

Foster drove competently, his eyes steady on the car ahead of him, sometimes directly behind, sometimes permitting two or three other cars in between, sometimes in a different lane. Beside him Peter shifted uneasily.

"He's not stopping in Manhattan at all!"

When they had gone through the tunnel both men were confused. They watched anxiously the movement of the station wagon ahead, once so close that Peter could see the painter's beard as he turned his head to reach for his cigarette lighter.

In downtown Newark, Miller signaled and pulled into a parking slot.

"Keep an eye on this guy. I'll have to park the car but I'll get back as soon as I can. Don't lose him, whatever happens."

While Miller was putting a coin in a parking meter, Peter got out of the car. Then the painter began to unload canvases. The building beside which he had parked was a run-down structure that should have been condemned twenty years before. According to the signs on the windows, it housed a barber, a dentist, a stamp dealer, and an art gallery.

Miller locked the car, picked up the four canvases he had removed, and went into the building. Following at a careful distance, Peter learned that the art gallery was on the top floor. There was no elevator. Apparently this thriving business did not encourage casual visitors. The unloading would probably be a long process.

On the street, within sight of Miller's car but out of range of his vision, Peter lighted his pipe and waited for Foster to return. It was nearly a quarter of an hour before he showed up. By that time Miller had already returned for a second load. There were only three more canvases to be delivered and he could handle those in one trip.

Peter was growing uneasy. He was beginning to wonder whether he'd have to tackle the painter single-handed and what excuse he'd have for it, when Foster came briskly down the street. Behind him were two neat, alert-looking men.

Foster spoke to them briefly and came up to Peter. "Reinforcements. Things are beginning to dovetail. They've been watching this place on another count. The ownership of the gallery changes every couple of months and some very odd customers drop in."

"Do you think Miller knows what he is mixed up with?"

"He'll know in about ten minutes, I should think."

As Miller came back to collect the last load of canvases, Peter turned his back. When the painter had gone inside, Foster nodded to the two neat young men who had closed in. "All right, let's go."

The four men climbed the stairs as quietly as they could and Foster eased open the door of the "art gallery."

Philip Miller had stacked the canvases against the wall and dropped into a chair to catch his breath. Behind an unexpectedly businesslike desk a stout man with rimless glasses and a sunken mouth was checking lists.

"You're out of condition," he told Miller who was breathing heavily. "Getting soft up there."

"All you do," Miller said resentfully, "is to sit back and—"

"—and take the risks." The other man spoke smoothly. "We can use four more of these next week. And we must have those new directives. Our sub-leaders are complaining that they have no clear course mapped out for them."

"I've been instructed to hold up all further deliveries for a month at least," Miller said sullenly.

"Why? You have to keep people stirred up. Strike while the iron is hot."

"It's too hot in Simonton. There has been a lot of trouble up there."

"Don't tell me the Boss slipped up!"

Miller was eager to shift the blame onto someone else. "I told him he was a fool to use that rifle. No one could have got into the place."

"Rifle! What's been going on?"

"Just people house-hunting, so far as I can make out. But he panicked because the printing press was there and shot to drive them off. Hit a guy too. We moved the stuff out that night. And what a job that was!"

"Shot someone, did he? That could be bad news. And what about the directives?"

Miller mopped his head. "He'll tell you himself."

"He doesn't tell us anything, my friend. He gives us orders." The eyes behind the rimless glasses were cold. "What happened to the directives?"

Foster walked into the room, followed by the two young government agents, with Peter bringing up the rear.

"We've got 'em," Foster said.

I

Peter had not returned to lunch though he telephoned Nancy later to tell her, somewhat cryptically, that all was going well. He expected to be home for dinner. It wasn't until after she had put down the telephone that she realized how tired his voice had sounded. Tired and drained, as though, with victory in sight, it had lost its savor.

During the afternoon, Noah, or Neil as he had at last become, took a walk, triumphantly accompanied by Max and Helen. When Nancy suggested that Neil bring Helen to dinner he refused, and then, after a look at Helen, he accepted.

"I want to see her entrance," he explained. "If she doesn't bring down the house I'll be surprised."

Nancy filled in part of that endless afternoon by selecting a dinner gown for Helen. Because Peter had seemed to like it, she chose for herself the gold dress which she had worn on her wedding night. By six o'clock she was ready and waiting impatiently, but still Peter did not come.

She was pacing the library when Murch announced Dick Stowell. He stopped in the doorway and whistled softly. "Are you taking in waifs and strays tonight?"

"Of course. Anyhow, I want you to know my brother. This is going to be quite an occasion. He'll be dining in public for the first time in nearly a year." She saw Dick's expression. "What's wrong?"

"I didn't know he—that is, Cynthia told me—"

Nancy flamed with indignation. "I heard about it from Helen Ferrell. She barged out there, looked at him, and ran. It was a cruel, filthy thing to do. But you needn't worry, Dick. He has discovered that he can cover the scars with grease paints."

"Grease paints!"

"He's a professional actor. Neil Carrington."

"Good lord, that guy! I heard he had disappeared, that there was some mystery about it. He used to be handsome, I understand. Never saw him myself as I don't go in much for Shakespeare."

"He is still handsome. He won't upset you."

Something in her hostile tone made him say, "Nancy!" He added, "Forgive a guy who is always putting his foot in it." Apparently her continued silence worried him because he came to take her hand. "Nancy? Still friends?" His eyes were intent on hers, watching her expression.

"Of course. I just don't want you to look at Neil as though he were something out of the Addams family."

"Nancy!" Without warning, he drew her out of her chair, into his arms; he was kissing her mouth, her cheeks, her eyes, her mouth again.

At first she was too astounded to move. Then she thrust

him away from her violently. He staggered against a chair, thrown off balance by her rapid action. For what seemed to be an endless interval they looked at each other.

"I thought you were Peter's best friend," she said bitingly. "The man he trusted more than anyone in the whole world."

Something of the contempt in her tone flicked him like a lash. He winced and caught hold of the back of a chair, his hands tightening, the color ebbing from his face.

"I'm sorry," he said. "Terribly sorry. I didn't mean to do that. But you're so beautiful."

"We had better forget it ever happened," Nancy said. As the front door opened, her face lighted up. "Peter's home!" Stowell still sagged against the back of the chair. "Pull yourself together, Dick, I won't have Peter hurt by knowing this."

Peter had gone upstairs to change and the library was quiet. Too quiet. At length, made uneasy by the silence, by the pain in Stowell's face, Nancy told him about the masked robber who had ransacked the library and knocked her out in Peter's studio. She touched the lump which she had tried to conceal under her hair.

"Good lord!" Stowell was aghast. "You say you didn't get a look at his face?"

"He wore a stocking tied around it, and a cap pulled over his hair."

"He might have hurt you badly. Whatever possessed you to go after him with a gun?"

"We've been having prowlers lately. And I wasn't half as frightened as I was angry. Anyhow, I shot him."

"You—what!"

She nodded. "There were traces of blood on the stairs so I know I hit him." As the outside door opened again she said, "That must be Neil."

Apparently Helen had been watching for him because Nancy heard their voices, heard Neil say, a new caressing note in his voice, "Hello, Kitten!"

Stowell groped in an inside pocket for his cigarette case, grunted impatiently, "I'm always mislaying the darned thing." He turned in surprise as the lovely girl

came in, followed by an exceptionally handsome man. To
achieve the effect he needed and conceal scars, Neil had
had to use a dark make-up that was almost bronze. He
looked as though he had just came from a vacation on a
Southern beach.

Nancy performed the introductions, noticed that Neil
was forcing Helen to take an active part in the conversation. As a rule, the actor was so accustomed to being the
center of attention, whether on stage or off, that he had
little awareness of other people except as an audience.
There was a new kind of gentleness in his manner, almost
humility. To Nancy's amusement, Helen accepted Stowell's obvious admiration as though she were accustomed to
men's attentions.

They talked easily until Peter appeared, still with that
air of weariness she had noticed in his voice over the
telephone. Although he was somewhat taken aback by his
unexpected guests he was impeccably courteous.

Nancy tried her best to show no change of attitude
toward Dick Stowell, for Peter's sake, but her manner had
lost much of its usual warmth and spontaneity. Everyone
tried hard but the dinner was constrained. It was a relief
when Neil refused coffee—"This is my first public appearance and now I have to go to bed"—and left the house. A
few minutes later Helen went up to her room.

Even when they had gone, the constraint remained.
Peter was called to the telephone once. On his return he
smoked his pipe and stared morosely into the fire. Stowell
groped for his cigarette case, grumbled, lapsed into
silence.

At length Peter said, "You look tired, Dick. Nothing
wrong, is there?"

"My plot got stuck. That's always a frustrating time for
a writer."

"It must be. I'll drive you home. It's a rotten night to
walk."

"Thanks a lot." Stowell looked at Nancy, his eyes imploring forgiveness. "Good night, Nancy, and thanks for
taking in stray dogs."

"Good night." She tried to speak warmly but her voice
was cold.

II

The two men were silent as Peter drove down the broad silent avenue. Peter's knuckles were white as he gripped the wheel.

It was Stowell who broke the silence. "Peter, I—" They were nearing his house now. "Peter, I must have lost my head this evening, just before you came home. I don't know how it happened but—Nancy's the most beautiful woman I ever saw. I got carried away."

Peter did not comment.

"She wouldn't give me the time of day, of course. She just reminded me that I was your best friend. That—hurt." The car had stopped before the house. "Peter, nothing has changed between us, has it?"

"What do you think?"

"You haven't answered the question, have you? You've asked one."

"It's early yet. Feel like a talk?"

Stowell's anxious expression lightened. "Sure," he said in relief. "Like old times." He unlocked the door and led the way into a combined living room and workroom, with a desk, typewriter, and neat piles of copy. "The new opus. I thought I had a sound plot but I'm afraid it's gone sour."

"I'm afraid so too, Dick."

Stowell's eyes leaped to Peter's.

"It started going wrong when I came up to Simonton, didn't it?"

Stowell eased himself carefully into a chair. "What on earth—?" He sounded bewildered.

"The funny thing is," but Peter did not seem to find it funny, "that when I was asked to do this job I said I didn't need any help. I said the best friend I had in the world was in Simonton. I said I could trust him with my life. I was wrong about that, wasn't I, Dick? Tonight, the FBI found the rifle with which you shot me. It was here in this house, under your bed. They found your cigarette case when they searched Morton's workshop late this afternoon, looking for the nice printing plant you moved out of the farmhouse. That must have been quite a job."

Stowell hardly seemed to breathe.

"They checked the type on your machine for similarities with that new bunch of typewritten directives you lost. Do you know where you left them, Dick? They had stuck to a newspaper you dropped in Hacker's office." He added almost casually, "Hacker doesn't like subversives either, whatever they may call themselves."

Stowell tried to straighten up, winced, put his hand up toward the pocket where he had constantly been groping for his cigarette case.

"Is that where Nancy shot you?" Peter asked gently. "You ought to see a doctor. Shall I call Ferrell? He is rapidly becoming an expert in gunshot wounds."

"What the hell are you talking about?" Stowell tried to get up.

Peter shook his head. "I'm not armed. I don't carry a gun against—my best friend. I'm talking about the story I heard from Philip Miller today. We—the federal agents and I—picked him up in Newark along with $50,000. We also picked up some information. Miller told everything he knew. And so, by the way, did Morton. I felt rather sorry for his wife. She hadn't known a thing about his activities."

Stowell was staring ahead of him, but he seemed to see nothing.

"Why did you come to the house tonight? To make sure Nancy didn't recognize you last night?"

Stowell said nothing at all.

"The queer thing is," Peter sounded very tired, "that the evidence against you stared me in the face from the beginning. You showed up as soon as I reached Simonton. You didn't believe my reasons for being here. You checked on my brother-in-law that night and nearly knocked me down. Even then I had a kind of awareness that it was you because of your size and power and speed, but I couldn't accept it. And there was also that rather grubby attempt, the night Nancy and I got here, to throw suspicion on Hacker. Just in case. So I was almost sure you were the brains behind this business, but I didn't want to believe it!"

There was a long pause. Peter went on heavily, "And then you shot me; you might have killed Nancy. But people don't matter to you, do they, Dick? Only power."

He got up wearily. "They'll be coming along to question you later tonight. I told them I'd rather see you first. Not that it matters much, I suppose. This is the end of the trail, Dick." He started for the door. "You'd better have a doctor look at you."

"Why? I'm through. Only I wish it hadn't been you, Peter. I hoped against hope that you weren't mixed up in this and I came to believe it. I was glad. You can believe that or not but it is true. I didn't want to shoot you."

"But you did."

"Well," Stowell said reasonably, "you got in my way."

TWENTY-ONE

NEXT morning there was a note on Nancy's breakfast tray. "It's all over," Peter had written. "I'll be busy today, helping to clear up the details. We have the men and the evidence is piling up. Did you guess that Dick Stowell was the top man? Dr. Ferrell had to probe for your bullet late last night but Dick will be all right—if that matters any more to him. He's finished. You can relax now. Tonight we can discuss our own plans for a change. Peter."

She looked at the note for a long time. It's all over. The last chapter. The end of the story. There was not a word, not a hint to suggest that Peter wanted her to stay. She knew that she did not have the courage to face him tonight, to talk casually about the annulment. For the first time in her life she wanted to run away from an unbearable situation.

When the maid came for her tray Nancy asked her to pack the suitcases she had brought with her, pointing out her original meager wardrobe. The other things no longer belonged to her.

When the maid had gone she called Neil. "We can leave today if you feel up to it. Peter has finished his job and—and—he doesn't need us any more. Max can pack for you and drive us down to the city."

There was a little pause and then Neil said, "Of course. Whenever you like. But I want to see Helen first. Oh, she's coming now. I'll call you back later, Nancy."

Neil opened the door for Helen. "Five minutes late," he told her severely

She smiled at him with new confidence and let him take her coat. "Are you going to read to me today?"

"No, I don't need a book this time." He stood looking down at her gravely and his voice soared in Marlowe's great invocation to Helen:

> *Was this the face that launch'd a thousand ships,*
> *And burnt the topless towers of Ilium?*
> *Sweet Helen, make me immortal with a kiss!*
> *Her lips suck forth my soul: see, where it flies!*
> *O, thou art fairer than the evening air*
> *Clad in the beauty of a thousand stars.*

Her eyes were shining. "Neil, you remembered it!"

"I remembered it." He tilted up her chin, kissed her mouth.

"Neil!"

"Helen, I need you. I love you. You've got to marry me—if I have to drag you off by the hair. Do you think—could you bear to be an actor's wife? I warn you it would be a long run. The rest of your life."

"Neil!" Her face was hidden against his shoulder.

He lifted her head, kissed her again. "I don't deserve you. You know that?"

The violet eyes were dancing. "Of course."

He laughed. "Don't you get out of hand, Kitten, now I have you so nicely tamed. When will you marry me?"

"But, Neil, we don't need to make plans right away, do we?"

"The thing is that Nancy and I are going back to New York today."

"Going—back?"

He nodded. "For good."

"I don't understand."

When he had told her the true story of Nancy's marriage and that the reason for it was gone, Helen said, "Oh, no, Neil! She loves him. You can't mistake it."

"I know, Kitten," he said soberly, "but that's the way it is. Peter has never even thought of her as a real wife; she was just his cover for the government job. But I want to talk about us. I'll get in touch with Windrom, the plastic surgery man, as soon as we reach town, and when I'm normal we'll be married."

"You're—I like you the way you are."

"Then come with us, darling. You can stay with Nancy until I'm out of the hospital. Will your father mind terribly?"

"He won't miss me, if that's what you mean. I told him last night I was going to stay here and, if you ever asked me, I'd marry you. Anyhow, the Gerards have been building him up so much that he's going to be a lot more than just a country doctor from now on. Everyone on the avenue will want to consult him. He'll probably be better satisfied than he ever was before."

"So that's all right," Neil said in a tone of satisfaction. He telephoned Nancy. "We're going to have a passenger."

"Helen? Oh, I'm glad, Neil! I'm terribly glad. I couldn't ask for a nicer sister. Whenever you are ready—"

The smile had vanished from Neil's face when he put down the telephone. "She is taking it hard," he said quietly. "Not about you, of course. She's delighted."

"It hardly seems fair for us to be so happy."

"Nancy has courage. Plenty of courage. That will carry her through." Neil turned as the door opened and Max came in.

"Mrs. Gerard says you'd like me to pack your stuff and drive you to New York."

"That's right. Hurry up, Kitten; go and get your things together. Max can collect them when he picks up Nancy's."

"Mrs. Gerard is going too?" Max was startled.

"That's right," Neil told him. "Mission accomplished."

I

"Mission accomplished," Peter said with a sigh of relief.

"The government owes you a debt of gratitude for this

job, Mr. Gerard," Foster said as he shook hands warmly. "Everything nicely wrapped up."

Nonetheless, the FBI man realized that Gerard had no feeling of satisfaction. The discovery that his best friend was his hidden enemy had cut deep.

"Someone had to do the job," Peter said.

"All I regret is that they rushed that new dipolmatic appointment. There was still time for you to take it."

"I don't regret that. I'm going to stay here and paint. Give myself a year, perhaps two years, to see if I really have the talent to succeed. If I don't have the stuff, I'll go back to the diplomatic service. But at least I'd like to find out."

"Good luck to you."

In spite of his deep regret over Stowell's betrayal, Peter felt unexpectedly lighthearted as he walked swiftly down the avenue toward his house. His mission was accomplished and he was free to devote himself, with a clear conscience, to the work he loved. He could hardly wait to see Nancy's pleasure when she knew of his decision. She was sure he had it in him to be a good painter. With her confidence behind him, he couldn't fail.

It was late but she would be waiting. He ran up the stairs. The door of Nancy's sitting room was open. He called, "Nancy!" When there was no answer he went in. The bedroom, too, was empty. "Nancy?"

His eyes fell on the envelope on the sitting room table, with "Peter," scrawled on it. He stood turning it over and over. At length he tore it open.

"Dear Peter, I'm glad everything has worked out so well, but, for your sake, I am sorry it had to be Dick Stowell. Now that Neil and I aren't needed any more, we are going back to town. When you want me for the annulment proceedings you can reach me through Dr. Warburton who will have my address. For the next few days he has most kindly asked us all—Neil and Helen and me—to stay at his house. I am truly grateful for your kindness to Neil. Nancy."

But she can't go, Peter thought blankly. She can't go. I counted on her.

After the first shock he tried to think. The loss of his

faith in Dick Stowell was a trifle compared with his loss of
Nancy. This was catastrophe. The life he had allowed
himself to dream of, when his mission was accomplished,
would be meaningless without Nancy.

The house was filled with her presence, her beauty, her
impulsive generosity, her laughter. And he hadn't, he
realized, given her much to laugh about. No trouble, she
had told him, could be worse than the trouble she'd
landed in by marrying him. A sacrifice to her brother.
From the beginning, that was what this marriage had
meant to Nancy.

When she had become so important, so essential, to him
he hardly knew. On their wedding night he had been
grimly amused at her locking her door. But since then,
moment by moment, he had found her more enchanting.
He had tried to keep the bargain he had made with her
but it had required all his self-control. Only when his job
was over would he be free to try to win her.

Well, he was free now, and she had gone.

Suddenly he shook himself, free of his despair. So far
he hadn't even tried to win her! He wasn't going to give
up the loveliest thing in his life without a struggle.

He telephoned Max who, after an interval, answered
sleepily.

"Sorry to get you out of bed, Max, but I want you to
drive me down to New York. To my wife."

II

The narrow house was dark when Peter rang the bell
two hours later. Rang and rang. At length a light was
switched on and Dr. Warburton, in dressing gown and
slippers, opened the door.

"What the devil do you mean by raising all that racket
at this time of night?"

"I am Peter Gerard."

"Oh. Well, I suppose you had better come in." The
doctor led the way upstairs to a library at the back of the
house, draperies open to reveal a dramatic view of the

East River and the lights of Long Island. He waved his uninvited guest to a chair. On another chair lay an open book. "I wasn't asleep." Shrewd eyes studied the young man.

"I understand you asked my wife and brother-in-law and—"

"—his fiancée. Glad to have them. I'm a confirmed old bachelor but I like having people around the house, and heaven knows there is plenty of room." He peered over his glasses. "I thought all Carrington needed was to snap out of his self-absorption and how right I was. And what a girl he's picked. A lovely child."

Peter cleared his throat. "I know it is rather late—"

The doctor looked at his watch. "The time," he said dryly, "is half-past one."

Peter flushed. "I suppose my wife is asleep."

"I certainly hope so." The doctor studied the drawn expression on Gerard's face and relented. "She is on the next floor, the room directly over this. But don't wake the whole house. Carrington needs rest to build him up for the next operation and the trip down to New York tired him."

"Thank you, sir, I'll be quiet."

Peter went up the stairs, tapped at the door.

"Who is it?" Nancy asked, startled.

"Peter."

A light flashed on. He open the door and went in, closing it behind him. Nancy had not undressed. She had been sitting in the dark, looking out of the window. Her eyes were brilliant with unshed tears.

"Peter, what's wrong? What on earth are you doing here at this time of night?"

"I came to take you home, of course." He sounded very angry.

"H-home?"

"You're my wife. Remember?"

"But, Peter—"

"I've brought you nothing but trouble, and shots fired at you, and a bashed head. You said yourself nothing could be worse than the trouble you'd had in marrying me. I just—I guess I took you for granted. But when I got back tonight and you weren't home, the bottom dropped out of my world. I was—lost. All this time I've been a blind fool. I knew you were beautiful and loyal and gallant. But only when you were gone did I know you were—you. The girl I love."

She shook her head slowly.

"You mean you don't—want me?" he asked.

"I mean—I thought you didn't want me."

"Nancy—about that wretched annulment—"

Again she shook her head.

"Then you'll come home with me tonight? As my wife?"

The answer was in her face. He gathered her close and kissed her as though he would never let her go. At length he said, his voice shaken with laughter and passion, "Get your coat. We're going home. Hurry."

"The New York house?"

"Tonight, yes. Tomorrow, we'll go back to Simonton. To stay."

"And to paint," she said.

"And to love. Forever. Come on, Nancy. I've waited a lifetime for you."

He reached for her coat and opened the door. As they stole down the stairs, hand in hand, Dr. Warburton watched them pass the lighted doorway where he stood. Neither of them was even aware of his presence. The outside door closed behind them. Smiling, Dr. Warburton returned to his book.